A PINK HOUSE ON WHEELS

A TWISTED ROLLER-COASTER OF ACTION,
SELF-DISCOVERY AND PASSIONATE LOVE.

By Tammy Bartaia

Sydney, NSW

DISCLAIMER

This is a work of fiction. All the names, characters, places, events and incidents in this book are the product of the author's imagination. Any resemblance to actual persons, living or dead, or actual events is purely coincidental.

"A PINK HOUSE ON WHEELS" Tammy Bartaia -1st ed.
ISBN 978-0-6454140-0-4

Contents

ABOUT THE AUTHOR

Tammy Bartaia is an international actress, TV presenter and author. From the age of seven, her dream was to become an actress. She studied screen acting at the National Institute of Dramatic Art (Nida) in Sydney, Australia.

Tammy had a burning desire to write a novel. She always loved to write. It allowed her to use her imagination to create something special. She never chases ideas, they come naturally to her. Everything she sees and touches reminds her of an idea and then it won't leave her alone until it has her full attention.

"Even when there is no pen and paper in my hand I always write in my mind," says Tammy.

"A PINK HOUSE ON WHEELS" is the second heart-warming novel from Tammy Bartaia. It's a twisted roller-coaster of action, self-discovery and passionate love.

Chapter One

Daisy glanced down at her wristwatch, it confirmed that she was punctual for the job interview. She arrived at the magazine publishing company at nine o'clock on the dot. She could hear the beating of her heart throbbing in her ears with excitement. Her palms grew sweaty and she wiped them on her skirt. Marching over to the secretary desk, she noticed the tall young woman spraying water onto the cactus, humming happily to herself.

"Hello, I'm Daisy Barton," she smiled at her. Tiny dimples appeared on both sides of her mouth.

"Just a sec, let me give my plant a quick drink," replied the secretary with a grin.

Daisy's eyes drifted towards the deep green mini cactus with tons of needless. The secretary moistened the soil quite well to make sure that the roots of a plant absorbed enough water. She gave a light spray under the pot as well. "This little cactus is my best friend here. It helps me breathe better and makes me happy."

"Yeah, plants really don't ask for much, just a splash of cold water and a bit of love." Replied Daisy.

The secretary placed the plant mister on the table. "What can I do for you?" She asked, fluttering her eyelashes. Daisy realised that her stiff, straight eyelashes looked exactly like insect legs.

"I have a job interview with the editor -in- chief," Daisy's voice filled with excitement at the thought of meeting Ms. Brown.

"She is going to be late today. Are you willing to wait for her or do you want me to reschedule your appointment?"

"No problem, I will wait for her," she gingerly perched herself on the edge of the chair. "I have been anticipating this moment for a very long time. Ms. Brown is my role model. I admire the fact that she had started her career from scratch and worked her way up until she fulfilled her dream." Daisy's eyes were blazing with passion.

"I really hope your job interview goes well," replied the secretary and crossed her fingers to express good luck.

"Thank you very much," said Daisy as she adjusted her high pony-tail. She leaned back on the black leather chair. Reaching into her hand-bag, she pulled out a tinted lip balm and applied a little as her lips felt chopped and dry. She caught her upper lip between her teeth, tasting her strawberry flavoured lip balm.

The secretary opened the window to let in some fresh air. The yel-low sun's rays streamed into the room. They were too bright to look at. Daisy stood up from her seat and approached the window overlooking a small park. Squinting up at the sky, she watched an airplane fly across the blue sky leaving white streaks. She closed her eyes and imagined herself sitting on a plane, escaping to the tropical island with mesmer-izing golden sandy beaches. Her pleasant thoughts were interrupted by the sound of approaching footsteps. She turned her head abruptly and saw the red- headed woman dressed in a burgundy suit, standing at the desk.

"I need my coffee now," she said to the secretary in a high-pitched voice.

"Sure, ma'am," replied the secretary energetically and ran into the kitchen to make coffee for her boss.

Ms. Brown was in her late forties. She had a collarbone length bob haircut, tanned skin and lots of freckles on her face and chest. Daisy stared fixedly at her as if she were a statue. Her eyes gleamed with ad-miration. Ms. Brown didn't even cast a glance at her. She walked through the narrow corridor leading to her room. The secretary ran after her holding a tray with a cup of coffee and some cookies.

A few minutes later, Daisy was called into Ms. Brown's office. She smoothed her hair with her hand and neatly tucked the front of her white shirt under the button of her jeans. Daisy knocked gently on the door. A feeling of both excitement and fear ran through her.

"Come in," said Ms. Brown in a cold tone.

Entering the room, Daisy's pale cheeks blushed due to shyness.

"Please, sit down and introduce yourself," Ms. Brown gestured to the chair with her chin.

Daisy sat down on the chair and put her legs modestly together. "It's truly an honour for me to be here." Her voice sounded strained. She gave a nervous smile, biting her lower lip.

Ms. Brown's eyes went to the round wall clock. "Dear, I don't have much time, could you please show me your current curriculum vitae?" She asked.

Daisy's grin faded. "Well, I have undergone short courses in journalism and media, but I have never worked as a magazine writer. I don't have any experience." She admitted. Her manner lacked confidence. Pulling the certificate out of the folder, she placed it on the table. Her fingers were slightly shaking.

Ms. Brown took a sip of her coffee before responding. "I have to be frank with you. Our magazine needs a team of   highly experienced strong writers. We are looking for someone who is capable to get the job done from day one. You need to learn a lot yet. I don' have time to train you. Unfortunately, I can't find a position for you."

Daisy realised that her lips were trembling. She pressed them together tightly in an attempt to stop them, but she wasn't able to hide her emotions. One fat tear rolled down her cheek from her left eye. Ms. Brown pulled a tissue out of the box and handed it to her.

"Wipe your tears, I hate seeing people cry. Let me give you a piece of advice, at a job interview do not apologize for the experience you don't have. You need to create a strong first impression. Have a confident smile, show your energy, enthusiasm and interest."

Daisy dried a tear with a tissue. "Thank you so much for your advice. Despite the fact that I didn't get the job, I'm very thankful to you for taking your time from your busy schedule to interview me for the position," she said and put her certificate back in the folder.

Ms. Brown stared at her for a moment, studying her face. "If you were representing a colour, which one would you be?" She asked.

Daisy shrugged her shoulders and glanced at her to see what did she mean by that comment. Ms. Brown drummed her fingers on her desk. "I would be the electric red colour. I'm fearless, determined and provocative. I suspect you would be the colour grey. It goes with everything, but it's very boring and invisible."

Daisy paused, collecting her thoughts. Her rebellious streak surfaced. The furrow in her brow didn't lift until she said what was inside her heart. "I don't agree with you, Ms. Brown. I may look grey on the outside, but I feel that my inner spirit is sky blue.

The colour blue is associated with imagination, freedom and open spaces," her tone left no room for argument. She stood up and walked towards the door very slowly as if the legs were hard to lift and move forward.

"Wait!" exclaimed Ms. Brown.

Daisy quickly turned her head. Ms. Brown gestured for her to come closer. Daisy took a small step forward.

"Well, I can offer you a position of a freelance writer," said Ms. Brown with a serious expression.

Daisy smiled through her eyes. Goosebumps ran down her body, giving the signal that something delightful was going to happen. Positive emotion overwhelmed her. Another tear streamed from her eye and fell into her hand. "Sorry, Ms. Brown, I can't stop crying," she gave a murmur of relief and wiped a tear with her hand.

"It's okay, I noticed that your tear fell from your right eye, it means happiness." Said Ms. Brown.

"Oh, I have never wondered which eye leaks first," she said, tears were still hanging on her long eyelashes.

Ms. brown chuckled softly to herself. Daisy smiled at her out of politeness. "It's been a while since a happy tear has fallen from my right eye." She said in a very low voice.

"Don't get too excited, dear. If you want to work with us, you should follow the strict rules. You need to work with enthusiasm and great deal of energy. You will have to write feature articles for our magazine. The articles must be well researched and well written before they make their way into the print. You have to focus just on your professional life and forget about your personal life. Before you decide to join us, please take into consideration that you won't get paid. If you prove to be a gifted writer then I will hire you."

"I understand, Ms. Brown. I'll do my best not to disappoint you. I can't thank you enough for giving me this opportunity," Daisy spoke too quickly as her excitement grew.

"You don't need to thank me, you just need to show me what you've got. You can start working tomorrow at nine o'clock. My secretary will give you a tour around the office building."

Daisy gave an appreciative smile. She put her hands together in prayer position as a thank you gesture.

Ms. Brown gave a small smile that didn't involve much movement of her lips. "Keep in mind that I'm an eagle-eyed boss," she said, pointing two V-sign fingers first at her own eyes, then at Daisy to signify-'I'm watching you!'

Daisy nodded her head in acknowledgement. Glancing at her closely, she realised that Ms. Brown's aquiline nose looked exactly like an eagle's break. A slow smile spread across her face. She walked towards the door with quick steps. She was light as a feather...

***

Daisy stepped out of the office building and took a deep breath. A light and pleasant breeze hit her face. She threw her head back filling her lungs with fresh air. She headed to the bus stop, humming a soft tune to herself. She was so distracted by her own thoughts that she failed to notice the yellow bus until the moment it drove straight past her. Daisy ran after the bus to catch it, waving her hand. The driver stopped and let her get on the bus. There were no empty seats left. Standing in the narrow aisle of a jammed bus, she grabbed the rubber handle loop to hold safely during her bus journey. The man on her left had an extremely unpleasant smell. His sweat smelled like vinegar.

When he lifted his hand to hold the loop, Daisy noticed the yellow armpit stains on his shirt. It made her feel sick. She tried to scoot over, but the man didn't let her. He was too busy listening to music through his headphone, bobbing his head up and down to the melody. Daisy covered her nose with her hand to get rid of the nasty smell.

Finally, the bus stopped right in front of her apartment building. She quickly tore the crowd and made her way to the exit. Daisy hopped off the bus, gasping for air. She realised that she had been holding her breath for nearly two minutes. As soon as she opened the front door to her apartment, the black dog with grey muzzle jumped up on her and licked her face.

Daisy laughed to herself. "I know you are curious to know if I got a job," she rubbed the dog's ears gently. "Yes, Sugar, I got a job!" She exclaimed in a proud tone. Sugar wagged his tail rapidly. She knew he was happy for her by the way he moved around in a wriggling mass of excitement.

Daisy hung her bag on a wooden wall hook and walked to the bathroom. She turned the door handle; the bathroom was occupied. "Dad! are you there?" She asked loudly.

"Yes, how did the job interview go?" He replied from behind the closed door.

"It went successfully. I have got an opportunity to become a magazine writer. I'm so happy I pinch myself to make sure that I'm not dreaming," her voice was full of joy and energy.

"How much is your salary?"

Daisy sighed softly. "Well, I won't be paid until I prove I'm worth hiring."

"Hm, so you work for free?" His voice dripped with sarcasm.

"Writing is my passion, Dad. My dream is to become an author."

"Wake up, stop dreaming. Get a real job!" He shouted.

Daisy heard the sound of a toilet flushing and then Robert opened a door.

Hot tears dribbled down her face silently. Without saying a word, she stepped into the bathroom and splashed her face with water. She couldn't stop her chin from quivering. Her father's heartless remark zapped her joy and energy. She stared at herself in the mirror. Her eyes were red and swollen, her button nose was chapped from sobbing. She was wallowing in self-pity. She swallowed a lump in her throat and closed her eyes, searching for strength in herself. Her expression momentarily froze. She remembered Ms. Brown telling her not to be the colour grey. Her inner self confidence instantly grew and let her be free from negative thoughts and self-doubts. She wiped her tears, exhaled her anger, pushed her shoulders back confidently and stormed out of the bathroom.

Daisy found her father sitting at the kitchen table, drinking beer from a pint glass. She folded her arms and looked at him straight in the eye. "I see that money is all you care about. One day I will become a famous writer and will pay you back every cent you spent on me. Just so you know, I will never ever give up on my dream." She said and seemed to mean it...

Chapter Two

First day at work felt exactly like first day at school. It was a bizarre mix of nervousness and excitement. Settling into a new job within a new environment was really nerve- racking for Daisy. Though she had a big smile on her face, she was very tense. Her heart was beating so fast, she was afraid it would jump out of her chest.

The secretary greeted her with a handshake. "Happy first day! It's so good to have you with us."

"Thank you very much for the warm welcome," Daisy's smile broadened into a grin until it crinkled her eyes.

The secretary guided her down the narrow corridor. Daisy could hear the keyboard clicking sound coming from the room ahead of her. She paused as if to savour the moment. Stepping into the room, she saw her co-workers sitting at their computers. They were moving their fingers across the keyboards super-fast, giving a pitter-patter sound of mechanical rain.

The secretary coughed softly to attract everyone's attention. "Hey guys, I'm pleased to announce that a new employee will start her journey with us. My gut instinct is telling me that Daisy will have a promising future as a writer. Please, be nice to her," she said, smiling. Then she turned her head to Daisy. "Let me introduce your co-workers- Grace and Leo to you. Grace is a celebrity gossip columnist. Leo writes articles about fashion trends for today's women. I hope you enjoy working with them," she winked at Daisy and gestured for her to sit at the table next to the narrow vertical window. Daisy smiled her thanks. The secretary walked out of the room and closed the door behind her.

Grace stopped typing, she looked up and studied Daisy's face intently for a moment. "Hi, newbie. Welcome to the team!" She exclaimed. When she smiled her double chin poked out.

"Thank you. I'm thrilled to be here." Replied Daisy.

Grace continued typing without looking at the computer screen. Daisy sat in her desk chair in a careful manner. She parted her lips to speak, but she felt a tickle in her nose and took a sudden quick breath in.

Her eyes became watery, her nose wrinkled up. 'Ah choo!' She sneezed through her mouth loudly. Spillage of saliva dripped off her lower lip. She quickly licked the spit with her tongue. "I'm sorry." She apologized.

"Bless you," said Leo and handed her a tissue.

Daisy sniffed and wiped her nose. "When I'm nervous I always get clumsy."

Leo gave a tight-lipped smile. The corner of his rainbow shirt collar flapped against his neck from the air flow coming through the fan. He fixed the collar on his shirt and said: "Don't worry, we will help you to get rid of your first day of work anxiety."

Daisy's eyes brightened. "Oh, really? Could you please enlighten me what are the do's and don'ts in the workplace?"

"Sure," said Leo as he crossed his legs. "Keep your eyes and ears wide open and mouth shut until you explore the lay of the land. Remember the names of the people you will come into contact with. Listen, watch and if you are uncertain about something, ask." Leo took a sip of water and gasped softly. He opened his mouth to say something, but Grace shushed him with a forefinger to her lips. "Now I will talk about don'ts," she leaned forward to Daisy. Resting her elbows on the desk, she cupped her chin in her hands. "Don't talk too much or too loud and don't laugh at everything. I say this from my experience. When someone asks you if you want some coffee- say yes, even if you don't like coffee."

Daisy chuckled softly. "You guys are so sweet and cute," she said in a relaxed tone. Reaching into her bag, she pulled out the hinged picture frame with glass front and placed it in the centre of the table. Leo almost broke his neck to get a close look at it. "Such a cool shot. How did you make the dog lick your face for a photo?" He asked in a surprising manner.

"Well, the vanilla ice cream was my secret weapon. I put some on my cheek to get the adorable kiss shot." Daisy chuckled at the thought.

As the wall clock struck twelve, Leo quickly shut down his computer. "Ding! Ding! It's a lunch break. "Let's hit the park," he suggested enthusiastically to his co-workers. The girls smiled in response.

It was hotter than they had expected when they stepped out of the office building. Leo rolled his shirt sleeves up. "Let's sit under the shade of a tree. I get sunburn very easily," he said and shielded his face against the sun with his hand.

"Fair enough, I also can't be exposed to the sun within a week after a laser hair removal treatment." Said Grace.

They sat under a big elm tree. It looked like an umbrella with wide spreading limbs and drooping branches. Grace bent her knees and folded her legs underneath her body. Taking the kebab sandwich out of her lunch box, she took a bite of it and chewed noisily.

Leo glanced at her ironically. "Enjoy your meal," he said and cleaned his hands with alcohol-based hand sanitizer. He started eating his green salad. Fumbling with the plastic fork, he tried his best to catch hold of the yellowish-green olive, but the olive refused to surrender. It kept falling from the fork. Leo gave up on trying, he put the fork aside and grabbed the plump olive with his hand. Taking one bite around the pit, he sighed in relief. His eyes drifted to Daisy. He noticed that she wasn't eating. "Are you okay?" He asked.

"My tight skirt doesn't allow me to sit in a comfortable position, actually I'm kind of sitting on one butt cheek," she said in a concerned voice.

Leo laughed. "I guess the best way to sit would be with your legs extended out in front of you, crossed at the ankles."

Daisy unbuttoned her skirt and got a little comfortable. She unfolded a sheet of aluminium foil and took out a French toast sprinkled with cinnamon. She lifted it to her mouth and was about to take a bite when she caught a seagull staring at her food with beady eyes. The bird had one leg pulled up and was limping and hopping on the other leg. Tilting its head to the side, the seagull opened its break wide, begging for food.

"Poor bird, it must have injured its leg," said Daisy. Her voice was full of sympathy.

She quickly broke her toast into bite sized pieces. The minute the bird saw Daisy let her guard down, it planted its leg firmly on the ground and strutted proudly on the grass.

In the blink of an eye, the seagull snatched the food right from her hand and flew away. It all happened so fast that Daisy had no time to react. Leo and Grace burst out laughing.

"The seagull conned you!" Leo exclaimed, still laughing.

"Such an opportunist bird," Daisy guffawed with delight. She took off her shoes and lay on the grass to rest a little. The grass tickled her bare feet. She looked down at the green carpet beneath her. She giggled and pointed her toes.

Leo threw himself backwards and landed on the grass. He put his dark grey backpack under his head, whistling softly to himself. "Hey, D, did you always want to work as a magazine writer?" He asked curiously as he rolled onto his right side to face her.

"My dream is to write a book." She said in a self-assured way. "Since my childhood writing has become my escape, a way to unburden heaviness of my mind."

"What do you want to write about?" Grace asked as she leaned back against the elm tree.

"Motherhood," replied Daisy with a thoughtful expression on her face.

"Motherhood?!" Leo and Grace exclaimed at exactly the same time.

"Unfortunately, I grew up without a mother. She passed away shortly after giving birth to me," Daisy sighed deeply, looking away.

Leo gently tapped her on the shoulder to show his compassion." I'm so sorry, dear," he said in a low voice.

"I've never felt love and care from my mother. My childhood was so dull and colourless. I want to have a baby one day in the future. My grandmother once told me that being a mother is like observing your heart move around outside your body."

"Did you already start writing your book?" Grace asked.

"Well, I want to tell a genuine story. I need to have a baby first to feel the joy of becoming a mother and then convey the divine emotion into writing." She replied.

"Oh, I don't plan on having kids until I'm forty," Grace stood and stretched.

Her remark made Leo smile. He put the empty plastic container in his backpack and turned to Daisy. "Thank you for sharing your story with us, dear. You seem to have a great deal of courage. Your father must be proud of you."

Daisy pushed herself up from the ground. "Actually, my dad doesn't care much about my dreams," she said in a broken tone and threw the leftovers in the green wheelie bin.

Leo felt awkward and lowered his eyes. After a short pause, he said: "Guys, lunch break is over. It's time to get back to work," he linked his arms with the girls and whisked them off to the office.

Entering the lobby, they bumped into Ms. Brown. Daisy froze to the spot, staring at her. She was astonished by her elegance. Ms. Brown looked majestic in a red tight- fitting bodycon dress. It hugged her hour-glass figure, enhancing her curves. She gave Daisy a stern look, pointing at her wristwatch with her index finger. "You are six minutes late," she said and curled her lips inwards, creating wrinkles above her top lip.

Daisy immediately dropped her gaze to escape the eagle eye of her boss. "I'm sorry, Ms. Brown, it won't happen again. I promise, " she said without raising her head.

Grace's cheeks were red from embarrassment. "I apologize for being late, Ms. Brown," she murmured.

Leo pulled his shirt collar up to help hide his face as he was unable to find the right words to excuse himself. Ms. Brown turned abruptly and walked towards the front door. Her black stiletto heels clip clocking on the marble floor. Daisy took a step forward to see her through the glass door. Ms. Brown sat in the maroon car and drove off. Daisy watched until her boss disappeared down the street. She felt uneasy after being scolded on the first day at work. She pulled a long face and slowly followed her co-workers up the stairs into their office.

Leo and Grace sat at their computers. They started typing fast, using all ten fingers. Daisy looked at them with great interest. "I can't increase my typing speed on the keyboard," she said, shaking her head.

Grace chuckled. "It takes practise, dear. It is very easy to learn where all the keys are. Typing fast allows me to quickly write my thoughts down and it saves my time," she replied and breezed through typing.

Daisy opened the blank word document. She paused, thinking hard and then she wrote the first line of her article. She felt so good inside of doing the thing that made her tick.

Leo leaned forward in his chair, so that he could read what she wrote. "If I may ask, who is Harry Barton?" He asked with curiosity.

"My uncle. He was a war hero. Uncle Harry was just twenty-two years old when he died in the war on terror in Afghanistan. He sacrificed his own life to save his fellow comrade. After his death, we received a medal of honour for his bravery on the front," said Daisy and raised her chin proudly.

"Oh, really? I felt goosebumps on my skin." Said Leo as he rubbed his arms.

"He was such a good human being. He loved to create poetry. He used to take me fishing and read his poems to me. I had really enjoyed listening to his beautiful poems. Even though I was a kid, I had learned some of his poems by heart. He had never shown his poems to anyone. I was for long his only audience. Now I want to write an article about uncle Harry and show his hidden talent to the world."

"Wow! Your article will go viral for sure." Exclaimed Leo.

She smiled warmly and continued typing until her workday was finished.

***

Daisy was greeted by her dog at the apartment entrance door. Sugar was so happy to see her after a gap of few hours. He gave a high-pitched bark and rolled on his back to express his joy. Daisy gently rubbed the dog's stomach in circles. "Are you hungry, Sugar?" She asked in a baby voice.

Sugar showed his approval by raising his ears. Daisy walked into the kitchen. Sugar followed her, wagging his tail. Daisy filled the bowl with the multi coloured kibble and added one tablespoon of yogurt to the dry pet food. Sugar ran to his dish and began eating right away.

Daisy glanced around the kitchen. She picked up the bread- crumbs from the table and wiped it with a damp washcloth. The sink was full of dirty dishes. Soaking them in the hot water, she soaped up her sponge. She scrubbed them under the water and washed off all suds.

She had a look of satisfaction when she completed her task. Wiping the sweat off her forehead with the back of her hand, she sank comfortably in a chair and took a deep breath.

The silence was disturbed by a buzzing sound of a black fly. It entered the open window and zoomed around the kitchen. The dog got annoyed and snapped at the air. He began barking so loudly that Daisy's father got alarmed and rushed into the kitchen, holding the shaving razor in his hand. His face was completely covered in soap. "What is happening here?" He asked.

"Everything is alright, Dad. Sugar was trying to catch a fly."

"Such a silly dog." Robert's voice filled with irony.

"Dad, I'm going to cook pasta for you."

"I'm not hungry, I just had an omelette," he replied and walked out of the kitchen.

Daisy followed him into the bathroom. Robert started shaving his face in the downwards direction.

"Dad, I'm working on my first article. It's about uncle Harry. I need your assistance in getting more information about him," she looked at her father with pleading eyes.

At the mention of his brother's name, Robert got startled and stumbled to his feet. The shaving razor fell out of his trembling hand. Daisy grabbed the razor from the floor and handed it to him. "Dad, are you okay?"

Robert nodded in response. Getting his breath back, he washed his face with cold water and got every last bit of soap off. Then he wiped his face with a waffle towel. "Harry was the favourite child of my parents. They had pampered his ambition, I meant nothing to them. When my mother received an official notification of Harry's death, she got a sudden heart attack and died," he said, growling. His cheeks flushed and his wrists formed into fists.

Daisy saw jealousy in her father's eyes. "I thought you would be eager to tell me inspiring stories about uncle Harry," sadness took a toll in her voice.

Robert stepped out of the bathroom. Avoiding her gaze, he pulled the railroad uniform from the front hall closet. "I don't have time for a chat, I have to go to work. I'm the bread-winner in my family," he said and put on his orange shirt with twin chest pockets. He clipped the ID badge with his name on it above the pocket on the right side of his shirt. Muttering something under his breath, he walked out the front door.

Daisy sighed deeply at the futile thought. She entered the small storage room and switched on the light. The room was filled with different sized boxes. She stumbled over the cardboard box full of years' worth of clutter. She always wanted to get rid of junk, but her father liked to keep things forever. Daisy stretched up on her tiptoes to reach the brown wooden box with rusty bronze decoration. The box was covered in dust. She blew the dust off and opened it. Pulling out the photos, she sat on the floor with folded legs. Her family heritage was displayed in front of her. She looked attentively at the black and white picture of her grandparents, holding hands with their sons, Robert and Harry. Even though the family portrait was faded, Daisy could easily read joy and happiness on their faces. She dug around the box and found the leather file folder. When she unzipped the folder, the five-pointed bronze star slipped off and fell into her lap. She stared in awe at uncle Harry's medal of honour.

The star was surrounded by a green laurel wreath, symbolizing victory. Daisy kissed the medal and carefully put it back in the folder. She briefly flicked through the army pictures of uncle Harry, dressed in the military uniform. He looked handsome with his chest puffed out with pride. Daisy quickly turned over the pages of her uncle's old notebook to find her favourite poem. It brought her into the old days at the moment she looked at it. She began to read out loud, following the flow of the poem's sense. She got lost in the creation of uncle Harry's feelings and thoughts. The last thing she pulled out of the leather folder was an envelope with a red kangaroo stamp in the top right corner. The envelope was labelled to: 'The hero soldier's family, from: Noah Irving, the hero's army buddy.' Daisy immediately opened it and looked inside. It was a condolence letter from the soldier, expressing his sympathy of the death of his comrade. Daisy turned the envelope back over and observed the return address. Noah Irving happened to live near her place of work. Her eyes sparkled with excitement as she discovered a person who could tell her the life changing war stories.

Chapter Three

Daisy stood at the bus stop awaiting the arrival of the bus. She was nervously tapping her foot on the ground as her nerves were fried by the prolonged waiting. The few buses arrived, but not the one she wanted to get on.

The sky turned dark grey all of a sudden and it started raining. Daisy stepped out of the bus shelter and allowed the sprinkling droplets to fall on her head. At first the rain felt light upon her body, then it became more intense. Her hair began dripping and within minutes went super curly. The cool rain made her refreshed on a hot summer day.

At last, the bus with the route number she needed arrived. She ascended the bus steps and found the seat by the window. The raindrops were hitting hard against the glass, leaving vertical streaks. Wiping the foggy glass with her hand, she looked through the window, so that she didn't miss her stop. It took her almost half an hour to reach the destination. She hopped off the bus and approached a sand beige house. For a few seconds her heart pitter-pattered in her chest. Taking a deep breath, she pressed the doorbell button. The bell imitated the crisp sound of birds chirping.

"Who's there?" Someone yelled through the door.

"Good afternoon, does Mr. Irving live here?" Daisy asked.

The door was cracked open as far as the security door chain permitted. "Yes, it's his residence," the middle-aged woman squinted for a better look. "Sorry, I couldn't recognize you. Is he expecting to see you? We weren't prepared for visitors," she spoke with her through the gap.

"I'm sorry I shouldn't have come to your house unannounced. I'm a magazine writer. I'm working on an article about war heroes." Daisy sounded nervous. Her voice was shaky and a little unclear.

The hostess lifted the chain out of the metal casing and opened the door. "You are wasting your time here. My husband doesn't talk to the media," she replied coldly and tucked her grey hair behind her ear.

Daisy felt a moment of disappointment as her expectations weren't satisfied. Her chin dipped to her chest. "I understand, I won't bother you anymore, ma'am," she said through tight lips.

Just when she gave up hope of seeing Noah Irving, a red -headed man slid into the hallway in a wheelchair. Daisy noticed that both of his legs were amputated below his knees. He was wearing military combat shorts and a button up brown shirt. Her face brightened with a smile.

"Hello, sir. My name is Daisy. My uncle, Harry Barton was," she paused for a moment as the man got teary eyed.

"A hero!" He exclaimed, interrupting her while she was speaking. "It's so nice of you to visit me. Please come inside, let me have a closer look at you," he said, wiping the corner of his right eye.

Daisy stepped into the wide hallway. Her eyes shone with pleasure. She bent down and wrapped her arms tightly around his shoulders. "I'm so glad to finally meet you." She said.

Mr. Irving kissed her on the forehead. "Your surprise appearance made my day, dear. I got slumped in a wheelchair, watching TV." He chuckled.

Daisy's eyes drifted towards the portrait of Noah and Harry hanging on the white painted wall. Momentarily she felt nostalgic. She had a longing feeling of the past when things seemed so much better. She wished to be six again, playing hide and seek with her uncle, listening to his stories and believing that magic was real.

Mr. Irving glanced at his wife. "Amalia, fetch us some tea, please," he said as he propelled his manual wheelchair to the dining room.

Daisy followed him. Her eyes scanned the room as she entered. The antique furniture made the room look like a museum. She glanced left and right, wide- eyed in surprise. She was amazed by the marble statues and carvings, stack of vintage books, hand carved dressers with slightly crooked drawers, carved and lacquered chairs. Daisy approached an antique oak chest with shabby leather straps and gently touched it. She had a feeling she connected to its creator who lived a long time ago.

"Please, make yourself comfortable," said Mr. Irving to her. His gruff voice broke into her thoughts. Daisy smiled softly and sat down in a large padded chair in front of him. The ceiling fan was spinning fast, pushing the air down and creating a cool breeze.

Mrs. Irving brought a large pot of freshly brewed green tea and two tea cups. She set the silver tray down on the table and handed the cup to Daisy. "Would you like some sugar in your tea?" She asked.

"No, thank you," replied Daisy as she blew hot tea to cool it.

"If there is anything you need, please don't hesitate to ask. I won't interrupt your conversation. I hope you will write a perfect interview article for the magazine," she grabbed the empty tray and walked out of the room.

Mr. Irving sipped the hot tea nosily. "So, you are a journalist, huh?" He asked.

"Well, I just got the first job as a magazine writer. You are my first respondent." Daisy replied modestly.

"Did you know that your uncle gave his life to rescue me?"

Mr. Irving's words gave her a sense of pride. Her dark eyes lit up with a gentle smile. Mr. Irving took another sip of his tea. "In spite of his own wounds, Harry threw himself in the path of rocket propelled grenade and machine gun fire to save me. It really was the terrible firefight," he said and let out a deep sigh. "I remember that day very clearly as if it happened yesterday," he continued. "I ran out of bullets. I thought I might not make it out alive, but Harry immediately ran towards me to protect me from the attacker."

"How did my uncle die?" Daisy interrupted him.

"My best friend was shot in the back by a sniper. He was face down in thick mud. I crawled over to him and dragged him across the stony Afghan riverbed. He was still alive, breathing only periodically. I held his hand and whispered in his ear: 'You are a real hero, mate.' He glanced at me for a moment, drew a sharp breath and then his heart stopped. I didn't even have a chance to cry over his death. In the blink of an eye, my legs were blown off and I got thrown into the air. I had a whooshing sound in my ear pulsing in the rhythm of my heartbeat," Mr. Irving paused. There was a tremble in his voice. It seemed he couldn't carry the burden of past memories anymore. Emotions overtook him and he cried his heart out. His tears carried a lot of pain and sorrow.

Daisy watched him in salience misty-eyed. The light-coloured, wispy hair on her arms stood up straight as she got chills all over her body. "Both of you are my heroes. I admire your loyalty, courage and strength." Her mascara dripped down her cheeks in tiny muddy rivulets. She wiped her tears with her hand and noticed the mascara smeared on her fingers.

Mr. Irving shrugged. His eyes crinkled at the sides slightly as he gave her a melancholy smile.

Daisy gulped down the last drops of her tea. "My uncle wrote beautiful love poems. His poetry is as mysterious as love itself. Did he share his poems with you?"

"His romantic poems were dedicated to the woman he was madly in love with. She was his muse. Harry used to keep her photo in his chest pocket. He was very careful not to crinkle it as it was the most precious thing he had."

"How did she look like?" Daisy asked with curiosity.

"I still remember her face. Her coal- black eyes were so pure and naive as if she were a newborn baby. Her thick braids were wrapped around the top of her head. It looked like a crown. She lived in Katoomba area in the heart of the magnificent Blue Mountains. Harry told me that she owned a tiny wooden house on wheels and he himself had painted it pink," said Mr. Irving with a thoughtful expression on his face.

"You described her so beautifully, I can vividly see her in my mind's eye. I think I will instantly recognize the muse of uncle Harry if I happen to meet her in the street."

Mr. Irving chuckled softly. "Would you like another cup of tea?" He asked.

"No, thank you. I'm afraid I have to leave now. I already took much of your time," she stood up from her seat.

"I hope I was useful for you, dear," he said as he ran his finger through his hair.

"Thanks a lot for opening your heart to me." Replied Daisy.

Mr. Irving gave her a double handshake as a gesture of trust.

***

Daisy started writing her first interview article with great enthusiasm. She had a feeling she was playing a hooky ring toss game with her friends, inventing new ways to play. She followed her editor's specifications and made the beginning of her piece catchy to keep a reader engaged. Daisy showed uncle Harry's creative world by displaying his talent for writing. She found the sincere way to say what was in the heart of a soldier. Sending the article to Ms. Brown, she felt great satisfaction in having completed a goal. She was elated, but after a few seconds, she realised that she wasn't really finished as she had to interact with her boss and defend what she had written.

On Monday morning Daisy made a trip to the office. Her heart fluttered briefly from excitement. Entering the building, she pulled a small mirror out of the bag and combed her hair with her fingers. Parting her hair to the left, she noticed that her fingernails were badly bitten. The skin around her nails was swollen. It seemed that nervousness and impatience made her bite her nails. Daisy balled her tiny hands into fists to hide her ugly fingernails and flew up the stairs, skipping every second step.

When her co-workers saw her, they began to clap their hands. Daisy looked at them with a puzzled expression on her face. Leo and Grace kept clapping and clapping. "Honey, you need to throw a party," Leo intoned jokily and handed her the latest issue of the magazine.

Flicking through the pages, Daisy found the title of her article 'Heroism, Comradeship and Love.' She blushed with contentment. Holding the magazine against her chest tightly, she looked near to tears. Grace gave her a bear hug. "Ms. Brown is waiting for you in her office," she whispered in her ear.

Daisy knocked timidly at Ms. Brown's door and poked her head into the room. Ms. Brown looked straight at her with her piercing eyes. "Keep up the good work," she said with a slight smile on her face.

Daisy let out a deep breath that sounded like a whistling of the boiling water coming from a kettle. Tension in her forehead was released as she allowed herself to relax a little.

With slow steps, she approached Ms. Brown's desk. "I'm grateful that you gave me a chance," she murmured and glanced at the stack of the magazines on the wooden table.

"I must admit that you exceeded my expectations, but don't let success get to your head. Just because you wrote a good article, doesn't mean you will get a permanent job immediately. You still have a long way to go."

"I know, Ms. Brown. I'm ready to face new challenges and work to the best of my ability." Daisy gave a promise.

Ms. Brown's smile widened a little. She seemed satisfied with Daisy's answer. "Take a day off from work today. Enjoy yourself." She encouraged her.

"Thank you so much. Can I grab two copies of the magazine?" She blushed as she asked.

"Sure," replied Ms. Brown. "By the way, you have a great story for a novel," she drummed her fingers on the table.

Daisy paused for a moment; her almond eyes sparkled with delight. She didn't know how to respond to her boss. She just nodded her head slowly and grabbed two copies of the magazine. She walked towards the door on her tiptoes to stop her high heels from making noise and quietly slid out of the room.

Daisy quickly ran down the stairs, positive emotions made her heart pound fast. She wanted nothing more than to put a smile on Noah Irving's face. She hopped on a bus and was at his place in ten minutes.

Mrs. Irving opened the door. "Oh, you again?" She smiled and let her into the house.

"I have a little surprise for Mr. Irving." Said Daisy.

"Just give him a minute, the doctor is checking his blood pressure."

"Is he okay?" Daisy asked in a concerned voice.

"He is fine. It's just a routine check-up."

Daisy's eyes roamed around the hallway. She glanced at her uncle's picture on the wall. It seemed to her that his smile was bigger as if he were proud of her.

Daisy's thoughts were interrupted by Mr. Irving's loud voice. "You must have really missed me, huh?"

She smiled broadly at him.

Mr. Irving was accompanied by a young tall man in a white coat with a stethoscope hanging over his neck. "Dear, let me introduce you to our family doctor, Eddie. He is very patient with me. He knows how to deal with cranky people."

The doctor laughed heartily; Mr. Irving laughed with him. "By the way, Daisy is a very talented journalist," he said and winked at her.

The doctor shook hands with Daisy. "Pleased to meet you," he said, looking straight into her eyes.

Her cheeks immediately blushed and she looked away. Reaching into her bag, she pulled out the magazine and handed it to Mr. Irving. "This is for you." She said.

Mr. Irving's eyes widened with interest. He opened the magazine and found himself famous. He almost fell out of his wheelchair from excitement. "With your permission, I'll read the article in my room. I need to be alone with my thoughts." Leaning on the hand rims with all his strength, he propelled himself to his room.

Daisy zipped her bag closed. She wished Mrs. Irving a nice day and took her leave. Eddie followed her outside.

"Where are you heading to?" He asked.

"I'm going to the bus stop." She replied.

"Oh, I hate public transport. Chronically late buses always lead to overcrowding. I prefer walking to driving a car. I'm never late or too early, I arrive precisely at the destination where I need to arrive."

"I also love walking. It's a good cardio exercise, but my workplace is far from my home. I've never walked such a long distance." She giggled.

"Walking regularly is very important for your health. You should think of it not as a duty but as a pleasant way to get from place to place. Let me walk you home and help you shake up your walking routine."

"Okay." Replied Daisy.

"Do you live alone?" He asked.

"No, I live with my father and my dog. My furry companion is so loving and compassionate. When I look into my dog's eyes, I instantly feel good."

"I bet your dog can sense that you are a good person. Even though he doesn't know the moral decisions you make, he can read your facial expressions."

Daisy blushed again at his compliment. She quickened her pace and stumbled on the uneven pavement. Eddie immediately caught her arm. Looking deeply into her eyes, he felt her breath under his neck. "I hope you are not hurt," he held her hand tightly.

Daisy quickly pulled her hand away as she was embarrassed to show her bitten fingernails. "I'm fine, thanks," she said and gave him a tight-lipped smile.

They walked along in silence. Her feet were sore when they reached the destination. "Thank you, Eddie, for your company. I guess I became a long-distance walker," she said, laughing.

"I'd like to see you again. Would you mind if we got together next weekend?" He asked.

"I'd love that," she said, lowering her eyes.

"Let's meet at the park near your place on Sunday. How does it sound?"

"Sounds good to me. At what time?"

"Let's say at around twelve o'clock."

Daisy nodded and crossed the road with quick, short steps. She gave him a hasty handshake. Eddie watched until she entered her apartment building.

Opening the front door, Daisy bumped into her father. "Dad, my first article got published!" she exclaimed, holding the magazine above her head. "Give it a read."

"I'm in a hurry now. I'm going to work," he replied shortly.

"No worries, I'll put it on your bedside table. You can read it later."

Robert shrugged. "But my vision gets blurry after reading. I even don't have time to visit an ophthalmologist," he stepped out the front door without saying goodbye.

Daisy breathed a sigh of concern. Removing her shoes gave her a sense of relief. She held the top of her foot in one hand and rubbed the length of the arch with the other hand. She massaged each foot, going from the heel to the arch. When she soothed the irritated nerve endings in her feet, she went to the storage room and put the magazine in the brown wooden box. Then she pulled out a photo of uncle Harry and said: 'You are still alive; I will not allow your memory to die.'

Chapter Four

Daisy couldn't stop thinking about Eddie. She needed to know whether she could trust him. 'What does this guy want from me? Is he just messing around? Is he after a one-night stand? Or maybe he found something interesting in me and wants to know me more?' These questions were circling in her head. She decided to put herself in a positive state of mind. Getting ready for the first date was very emotional for her. She wanted to make herself effortlessly charming. Daisy neatly painted her short nails delicate shade of red. She chose a bold, 'look at me' colour as she wanted to show Eddie her daring, outgoing side. She blew on her painted nails to speed up the drying time. Humming softly to herself, she created an elegant low bun with the help of a hair donut. Daisy didn't spend much time putting on makeup. She knew that foundation would look cakey and broken in natural light. She just applied some mascara, blush and pink lip gloss. It made her complexion look healthier. Opening the closet door, she grabbed her favourite pink pleated dress with a white bow knot belt.

Daisy used a trick not to mess up her hairstyle while getting dressed. She pulled a large square scarf over her head and carefully put the dress on. Then she pulled the scarf off and managed to keep her hairstyle looking good.

"Do I look pretty?!" She exclaimed as she grabbed the picture of her mother from the wall shelf. "I know you are happy to see me in your dress, Mom," said Daisy and spun around holding the framed photo against her chest. She had a feeling she received her mother's blessing.

Stepping outside, she put on her sunglasses to shield her eyes from the bright sunlight. Although it was hot, a gentle breeze kept her cool.

Daisy didn't walk far before she reached the park. She noticed Eddie from a distance. He was leaning against the eucalyptus tree. His puffy curly hair looked like sheep's wool. She waved at him and gave a sweet smile. Eddie waved back. Daisy lifted her cat eye sunglasses to her head. "I hope I'm not late," she said and inched closer to him.

"You seem to be fairly punctual," he replied and kissed her cheek.

"Well, punctuality teaches me the essence of time and makes me aware of its value," she tapped gently on her wristwatch.

They walked slowly in synchronized steps along the shore of the small lake. The dark brown ducks were chilling by the water. They were surrounded by the tiny ducklings with fluffy feathers.

Daisy paused and gazed at the lake with smiling eyes. The ducklings were making a funny 'quack quack' sound. Pulling a slice of bread out of the plastic bag, she tore it into small pieces. Then she threw out some bread crumbs for the ducks to enjoy. Nearly a dozen ducks gathered around her. "Oh, I don't have enough food for them," she said in a tone of regret.

Eddie laughed. "Perhaps it would be better if you didn't give the bread to the ducks that fight, just feed the tiny ducklings."

Rolling up a small piece of bread into a ball, Daisy threw it out into the lake for the ducklings. "When I was little, I used to visit a pond after school to feed the ducks. They were so cute and friendly, I even gave names to them." She chuckled.

Eddie gazed intently into her eyes. "There is no doubt that you are the most gentle and caring person I've ever met."

"You are making me blush," replied Daisy with a wave of her hand and a soft smile.

He interlocked his fingers with hers.

They continued their walk through the park. A slight breeze brushed her rosy cheeks. Daisy slipped off her sandals as she wanted to walk barefoot on the grass. The blades of grass gently tickled her ankles. She enjoyed a soft and somewhat prickly swath of green beneath her feet. "The fresh air, sunshine and green environment make me feel happier. I'm in tune with nature," she said and flopped down in the grass.

Eddie lay down next to her. "I must confess that I really like you, Daisy. You are my dream girl," he said with a serious expression on his face.

Daisy was flattered by his compliment. She felt a warm glow inside. "What do you like about me?" She asked without looking at him.

"You are a perfect woman. I'm captivated by your beauty and intelligence. I love your drive and ambition. Mr. Irving praised your talent. He thinks you will go far with your determination."

Daisy's eyes sparkled with joy. "I guess in life there is no challenge which we can't overcome if we are really determined." She pushed her hair off her face, trying to fix herself in front of him.

For a moment Eddie was too stunned to say anything. He stared at her as if he were staring at a rainbow and it was so pleasing to his eye he didn't want to look away. Then he smiled and said: "You are absolutely amazing. You just revived my faith in women."

Daisy blushed from her neck to her hairline when he praised her. "What is your perception of relationship?" She asked.

"Open communication between partners and compromise from both sides," he replied without much thought. "You know, my ex-girlfriend failed in a small and big ways as her determination was never strong enough," he shook his head. "What does relationship mean to you, dear?"

"It means having a bond with someone with whom you can be your true self and stick with that person through thick and thin. I would give my all for true love." She admitted.

Eddie took her hand in his. She had a self-satisfied smile on her face. Perfectly painted nails boosted her confidence. Eddie kissed her hand softly. "I think we are like minded souls, dear. I'm also very determined and ambitious. I want to open a private hospital, it's my long-term goal. One day I will be a very successful doctor and I know I will have an ideal family," he said and seemed to believe in himself.

Daisy looked at him with her mouth slightly open. She was impressed by his unshakable assurance. Eddie touched her chin with back of his fingers. He snuggled close to her and gently kissed the corner of her heart -shaped lips. Daisy blushed again and grinned. She had never been so close to a man before. Even though she felt comforted in the warmth of his care, she was a bit scared of being too vulnerable. She slowly stood up and stretched her arms above her head. Eddie rose up on one elbow. " Let me help you with your shoes," he said, smiling.

"You are such a gentleman," she replied, pulling her foot out.

He put her white leather sandal on her right foot. "It fits on you perfectly, Cinderella!" Eddie exclaimed. He could tell she was happy with him by her hearty laugh.

"I really enjoyed spending time with you, but I'm afraid I have to go home now; I need to feed my dog," she said, apologetically.

He wrapped his arms around her waist and whispered in her ear: "Promise me that you will meet me here next Sunday."

"You have my word," she said and kissed his cheek. She slowly freed herself from his arms and ran through the trees, giggling...

When Daisy entered the office the following day, her co-workers felt there was something different about her. Her smile was broad, creating dimples in her cheeks, her eyes shone like the sun gold coins. Her glowing face made it obvious that she had enjoyed her weekend.

Leo hesitated a moment and then the habitual curiosity got the better of him. "Come on, girl, tell us what is hiding behind your happy face," he said, leaning forward over the table.

Daisy smiled, her teeth teasing her lower lip. She spilled the beans about her date. Grace got very excited by the news. "Is your doctor hot or cute?" She asked, grinning.

"Well, he has a sweet personality. He is cute with slightly plump cheeks and freckles. I really had fun interacting with him."

Leo took a sip of water and said: "I'm crazy about baby-faced men. I will do my best not to steal your boyfriend."

The girls laughed out loud.

***

The second date was very important for Daisy. She knew it would give her a true sense of Eddie's love potential. Daisy was happy that their shared interest has been established, she just wanted to make sure that there was a real chemistry between them. She was ready to let her guard down and reveal her true self with him.

When she saw Eddie standing at the entrance of the park, she became euphoric. She had a feeling her heart was pumping away. Eddie handed her a bouquet of fresh cut daisies. "I saw these beautiful flowers and thought of you."

Daisy gave him a half smile. "It's a nice gesture from you, but I think every flower should blossom in nature. They cry when they are cut, we just don't see it. That's why I don't like flowers in a vase."

"I have never thought about it that way. I will never cut flowers again. I promise," he replied and looped his arm through hers.

They went for a walk in the park. "I missed you," he said and gave her a long stare.

"I missed you too," she replied with a smile. The blood rushed to her cheeks and made them rosy.

"By the way, I told my parents about you," he gave a rakish smile as he blushed.

"What exactly did you tell them?" She asked.

"I told them that I found a potential partner. A girl who fits my criteria which includes matching of my thinking and goals in life. My parents live in New Zeeland. Unfortunately, I can't introduce you to them now."

"I would love to meet them one day," she said excitedly.

They approached a giant oak tree. The sun's rays were shining brightly through its large branches.

"Look, someone has curved a heart on a tree trunk," she pointed to the big carved heart with an arrow.

"It's so romantic. Let's put our initials in the heart," he said, sliding his hand in his pocket to pull the key out.

Eddie began carving the letters- D and E on a tree trunk. The key wasn't sharp enough, so he put a lot of effort in his job.

"The heart is a symbol of love and unity," he said, proudly.

Daisy smiled and nodded in response. Eddie cupped her face in his chubby hands. "Before expressing a feeling, I needed to know what was it. I spent alone some time thinking about you," he kissed her earlobe tenderly and whispered: "I realised that I fell in love with you at first sight."

Daisy closed her eyes and pursed her lips. Eddie gently touched her lips with his. She breathed in the woody scent of his cologne. Her lips parted slightly, letting him slide his tongue into her mouth. He ran his tongue along the roof of her mouth. The pleasure of a passionate kiss was disturbed when the thick raindrops fell on their cheeks. They laughed at the awkward moment.

"Let's get out of here until we get soaking wet," said Eddie, wiping the raindrop from his chin.

They ran hand in hand through the outdoor shower. Pouring rain made her feel delighted. She kept laughing carelessly. He laughed with her.

A few minutes later, the rain stopped. A damp smell lingered in the air. It was strong and sharp, but also earthy.

"I had so much fun today," said Daisy with childish enthusiasm.

Eddie didn't respond, his eyes were drawn to her chest. Daisy looked down at her shirt. She realised that the rain made her white shirt transparent and let her nipples show through it. Eddie quickly withdrew his eyes as he didn't want her to feel uncomfortable. Daisy gave him a bashful smile. "I better go home now," she said. Her bare arms prickled with goosebumps.

"As you wish, sweetheart. I will see you next Sunday."

"At our secret spot." She giggled.

"No, my dear. Next time I will pay you a visit. I'd like to meet your father."

Daisy was puzzled. "Really?" She asked, picturing her father's face if she told him about Eddie.

"I hope you don't mind my initiative," he said with pleading eyes.

"No, not at all. You will be welcomed," she replied and shielded her chest with her purse.

Wearing the wet clothes made her shiver. She rubbed her goose-pimpled arms.

The raindrops were still dripping from her hair when she stepped into her apartment. Her father was sitting on a small wooden stool in the hallway, polishing his black leather shoes. Daisy plugged her nose to avoid the strong smell of shoe polish. Robert glanced up at her and knitted his eyebrows together. "Where have you been?" He asked in a stern voice.

"I took a stroll in the park with my friend."

Robert continued polishing his shoes with the brush in small circular motions, allowing the polish to sink deep into the leather. He seemed to be very careful not to get any shoe polish on the floor as he used an old newspaper as a protective barrier.

Daisy cleared her throat loudly. "Dad, I need to tell you something," she said, her voice was strained.

"Are you in trouble?" Robert started buffing the leather with a soft cloth, making back and forth movements to add glossy appearance to his shoes.

Daisy shook her head side to side as a way of saying no. "I just met someone and I think I'm falling in love with him. He is a very nice guy. He wants to meet you in person," she paused to see her father's reaction.

His face turned red. "Bullshit! There is no such thing as love at first sight. He just wants to seduce you and get into your pants. If you make yourself seem too available to him, he will lose interest in you." Robert gave an angry sigh.

"Then why is he willing to meet you?!" She exclaimed in disbelief.

"He just wants to make you his sex toy and he needs to have my approval," he yelled hysterically.

Daisy realised that there was no point talking to her father. She walked past him without saying a word. Entering the bathroom, she slammed the door. She peeled off her wet clothes and jumped into a hot shower.

***

It was Sunday morning. The alarm clock buzzed indicating nine o'clock in large red numbers. Daisy hit the snooze button and jumped off the bed. Sliding her feet into fluffy slippers, she marched to the kitchen. Robert was reading a newspaper while drinking black tea. Daisy poured herself a cup of coffee. "Dad, my boyfriend will come over for dinner. Please, be nice to him that's all I'm asking for."

"Hm, dinner," he said sarcastically and arched his eyebrow. "Who is going to cook?"

"I will cook pasta in delicious tomato sauce."

Robert didn't say anything. He took a big gulp of his tea.

"And one more thing, Dad, I want you to wear the green shirt I ironed yesterday," she said and without waiting for a response walked out of the kitchen.

Daisy spent several hours on household chores. She cleaned floor space in the dining room with a lightly dampened mop as she wanted everything to look shiny. Then she began vacuuming the furniture with a side-to-side motion and short strokes. The vacuum's high frequency sound made her dog annoyed. Sugar attacked the vacuum baring his teeth.

He tried to show the provoking monster who was the boss! Daisy bribed the dog with a treat to keep quiet and let her do the job. When she finished vacuuming the rug, the dog followed her to the kitchen. Daisy donned a full-length polka dot apron over her dress. She hummed to herself the same melody all day long quite unconsciously. She turned fresh tomatoes into homemade tomato sauce. Inhaling its aroma, she stuck her finger in hot sauce and put it in her mouth. "Yum!" She complemented herself for the effort.

As soon as the clock struck six, Eddie appeared on her doorstep. Daisy welcomed him with a warm hug. He handed her a bottle of wine. "I feel nervous and excited at the same time," he said in a low, almost inaudible tone.

"It's just dinner. Please, relax." Daisy took his hand and guided him into the dining room.

Robert stood by the window, looking out. He was wearing the green shirt his daughter wanted him to wear. When he heard footsteps approaching him from behind, he turned around.

Daisy cast a rapid glance at Eddie. "Let me introduce you to my father, Robert."

Eddie stretched out his hand to him for a handshake. Robert squeezed his hand so hard, that Eddie couldn't wait to pull his hand away. He smiled for the sake of politeness. "Nice to meet you, sir." He murmured.

Robert nodded his head. Giving him any icy glare, he tried to overpower him. The tension in the room was palpable. When the dog saw the guest, he immediately started barking. Daisy petted the dog to calm him down. "It's so weird, Sugar never barks at guests," she said in a concerned voice.

"I hope I will make friends with your dog," Eddie said, smiling.

"Please, make yourself at home," she winked, encouraging him.

Eddie pulled up a chair and sat at the table. A round dining table with lion claw feet was covered with the white lace tablecloth. Daisy's signature dish was served in a large bowel. She put spaghetti on one fourth of her boyfriend's plate and poured a generous spoonful of tomato sauce on top.

"Thank you. It smells delicious," said Eddie as he spread the napkin over his lap.

Robert plunged his fork into his spaghetti. His eyes were glued to his food. Daisy handed a wine bottle to Eddie. "Could you please open it?" She asked him.

Eddie placed a knife under the lip of the bottle and started turning it until he pulled up the cork.

"Good job!" Daisy encouraged him.

Eddie smiled broadly and poured red wine into the glasses. "I'd like to propose a toast to our friendship. Thank you, Mr. Barton for opening your home to me," he said and blushed, discomfited by Robert's eyes staring at him.

After an awkward silence, Daisy lifted her glass: "Cheers to friend-ship and love!" She exclaimed. She gave her father a quick glance and then looked away.

Robert emptied his glass and continued chewing his food slowly. Daisy and Eddie exchanged looks, communicating with their eyes. Daisy arched her eyebrows accompanied by a smile, showing affection. Taking a cue from her, Eddie turned towards Robert and said: "Mr. Barton, I need to express my love and admiration for your daughter. She is the most beautiful, intelligent and loving woman I've ever met," he took a gulp after gulp of wine until his glass was empty.

Daisy noticed that his hands were shaking. Tension built up in Rob-ert's facial muscles. Grinding his teeth, he clenched his jaw. "You are wrong if you think you can win my heart with beautiful words, young man," he said and poured himself another glass of wine.

"Mr. Barton, I feel really offended that you don't trust me. My in-tentions towards your daughter are serious."

Robert stood up from his chair. "I don't trust anyone. You shouldn't waste your time convincing me," his voice was harsh.

Daisy felt embarrassed. Eddie's furrowed brows told her that he was very concerned. She didn't know what to say, she just twirled the spa-ghetti around her fork. Eddie quickly stood up from his seat. He pulled a blue velvet box out of his pocket and opened it. Daisy was wide eyed in amazement when she saw a tiny diamond ring. Eddie glanced at Rob-ert in an effort to read his expression. "Sir, do you believe me now?" He asked.

Robert's nostrils flared outwards, his lips tightened and his face flushed red with rage. He gave a deep sigh and walked out of the room without looking back. Daisy stared at Eddie for a moment. Her eye-brows were raised and slightly curved. Her mouth hung open. "Wow! What a surprise." She exclaimed.

Eddie took the diamond ring out of the box. "This ring is a symbol of my commitment to our relationship," he said, placing the promise ring on her finger.

Daisy glanced down at the sparkling diamond. "I absolutely love this ring. It fits perfectly on my finger," her voice got shaky.

Eddie kissed her hand gently. Daisy's lips curved into a soft smile, showing empathy. "Eddie, I would like to apologize on my father's behalf."

"No worries, I know fathers are overprotective of their daughters. They want to save them from the evil boys," he said, laughing.

"You are so understanding," she gently touched his face.

"Sweetie, I'm gonna take off now. I have got a super busy working schedule, so I will see you next Sunday. Mr. Irving invited us to his house."

"Really?" She asked with more energy in her voice. "I miss him so much."

"And I will miss you like crazy as soon as I step out the front door," he gave her a goodbye kiss and left.

From the minute Eddie put a ring on Daisy's finger, she couldn't stop staring at her left hand. Everything happened so fast, she didn't have time to process any of it. Momentarily she was confused between what she wanted and what she was supposed to do. She inhaled deeply, trying to get an answer from herself regarding what she felt inside her head and heart. Her mind knew that Eddie was right for her, but her heart had sweeter excuse not to follow her mind. She was scared of commitment as it would be an end to her independent life. Curling up on the coach, she closed her eyes and allowed herself to fantasize about being Eddie's wife. She wondered how nice it would be to do romantic things with him: watching the sunrise together, kissing and cuddling up by a warm fire and roasting marshmallows, go for a hot air balloon ride, swim with the dolphins. Chuckling at the thought, she imagined holding a newborn baby in her arms. The desire to become a mother was so strong that she instantly got rid of her doubts.

When Daisy woke up, she glanced at her diamond ring with a twinkle in her eyes. She was cautions not to get the ring caught on anything that could damage it. She carefully buffed it with the jewellery cleaning cloth and smiled contentedly to herself.

On the way to her office, she kept her fingers on display, trying to draw attention to her ring. She held her left hand facing her chest, so that passers-by could get a good view of her diamond ring.

When Leo and Grace saw her ring, they almost fell off their chairs. Daisy shared her good news with them in a very enthusiastic manner. While talking she used her left hand more than usual, showing off her rock.

"I'm happy I found my Mr. Right." She said with confidence.

"What is the most attractive thing about him?" Grace asked her.

Daisy paused and thought for a moment. "He is not afraid to commit."

"It means he is husband material." Replied Grace.

"Exactly," said Daisy, smiling.

Leo stood up from his seat as he heard echoing footsteps in the corridor. "Shhh! He exclaimed. "Ms. Brown might hear us." He said in a very low voice.

Daisy got startled. She quickly hid her ring in her pocket and stared at the computer screen.

'Can Love at first sight really lead to a lasting marriage?' It was the topic of her new article. She started writing about making a connection with someone as soon as you meet. The moment when you first see each other and you realise that nothing else matters around. Daisy was focused on explaining the electricity type of feeling that is a result of a special connection between two people. Writing down her thoughts and feelings helped her understand them more clearly and gave her control of her emotions.

***

The week has passed quickly. Daisy was eager to visit Mr. Irving's place. She moved impatiently to and fro in the hallway until the clock struck five. Stepping out of her apartment building, she inhaled the mild sweet honey smell. The jacaranda trees in full bloom were lined up along the street. They resembled upturned umbrellas. Daisy walked on the fallen flowers that made a carpet of pale purple. She picked up the trumpet shaped flowers off the ground, enjoying a flawlessly purple moment.

It was nearly six when she reached Mr. Irving's house. Daisy rang the doorbell and her heart began to pound. Eddie opened the door with a big smile. "I knew you would come on time," he embraced her and gave her a peck on the cheek. Pursing his lips, he made a smacky mwah sound. He threw his arm around her shoulder and walked her into the dining room.

Mr. and Mrs. Irving were sitting at a dinner table. Daisy greeted them with a friendly 'Hello!'

Mr. Irving popped the cork on a champagne bottle. Tiny bubbles rushed out of the bottle like shooting stars. The host poured the champagne into waiting flutes. The glasses were clinked and everyone cheered loudly. Daisy enjoyed the bubbles dancing in the glass. The droplets of liquid crushed against her tongue. She tasted the powerful flavours of citrus, herbs and toast. Golden drink made her giggly and light headed.

Mrs. Irving impressed everyone with her culinary skills. The roasted turkey with lemon and garlic herb butter was mouth-watering. Daisy plunged her fork into the dish. Momentarily she held a small piece of turkey breast in her mouth. Its tender and moist texture gave her pleasure at the very first bite. "I've never tasted such a delicious dish since my grandmother died," she said. Her voice was filled with nostalgia, her eyes misted over. Everyone could easily see the floating memories through her head.

Then, just a few minutes later, Eddie got down on one knee in front of Daisy. "Will you marry me?" He asked her in a trembling voice. His cheeks were cherry red.

Daisy had a sudden choking cough. She felt as if something stuck at the back of her throat. Eddie handed her a glass of water. "Relax, dear. I think nervousness caused muscle spasms in your throat." He said and gently tapped her on the back.

Daisy emptied the glass with one swallow. "I'm sorry," she said as she inhaled deeply.

Mr. Irving smiled at her, expressing his support. "Daisy, you don't need to respond to a marriage proposal right away. Just listen to what your heart is saying." He said sincerely as a friend.

Daisy took Eddie's hand into hers and said: "My answer is yes!"

Eddie pulled her closer to him until their lips touched.

"Congratulations to the future bride and groom!" Exclaimed Mr. Irving and clapped his hands in excitement.

The happy couple left the house in high spirits. Eddie put his leather jacket around her. "It's a bit chilly outside." He said.

Daisy smiled; she was pleased with his nice gesture. "I love walking after eating," she said, giggling.

"I take a twenty-minute walk after dinner every night. It's a great way to help digestion. I will help you start a healthy lifestyle when you move into my house," he said and squeezed her hand two times, trying to say 'I want you.' There was a slight pressure in his touch. She saw a sparkle of horniness in his eyes. Daisy blushed as she realised he was aroused by her.

"I want us to get married as soon as possible," said Eddie and focused on her eyes.

Daisy smiled, giving him a silent assurance.

"To be honest I don't see a point of a huge wedding. I would rather spend money going to a honeymoon resort." Said Eddie.

Daisy paused for thought. She had planned her fairy tale wedding way before even she met him. Her dream was to get married in a church. On her special day she wanted to wear a beautiful white dress and feel like a princess. Despite her strong desire to have a big wedding, Daisy agreed to him in all matters.

She didn't want to spoil Eddie's mood, so she smiled broadly and said: "There is nothing more memorable than a romantic holiday."

"Let's have a civil wedding at a courthouse. We can skip the guest list completely and just invite two witnesses to the ceremony to sign the marriage certificate." He suggested.

"I have a small request." Said Daisy.

"I'll do anything for you, dear." He replied.

"Can we have four witnesses at the wedding ceremony? I can't choose between my two friends."

"Of course, my love. I will invite Mr. Irving and his wife."

She nodded in agreement.

While they were busy making their future plans, they reached Daisy's place.

"Tomorrow I will make an appointment at a registry office and arrange the wedding ceremony," he gave her a long and tight hug. "I don't want to let you go. I hate saying goodbye to you."

"Soon we will always be together. Nothing will keep us apart," she said, pulling her keys out of her purse. She gave him a quick kiss on the lips and entered her apartment building.

Daisy turned the key into the lock and opened the front door. The sound of keys rattling made the dog scared. Sugar started barking and growling.

"Be quiet," she shushed the dog with a wave.

Daisy's father was snoring so loud, she could hear it two bedrooms away. She removed her shoes and tiptoed into her room. Sugar followed her. Daisy put on her long t-shirt and lay in bed, tucked warmly under the cotton blanket. The dog stared at her with big brown eyes expectantly. Daisy guessed the stare was his way of claiming ownership of her resting place. She chuckled softly and gave him a hand signal to jump up on the bed. Sugar nuzzled up against her, giving her a sign that he was ready for petting. Daisy scratched the dog behind his ears. Sugar curled up into a ball next to her. Daisy kissed the dog on the head. "Once I get married, I won't be able to see you every day. I will miss you so much," she sighed.

Tears streamed down her face as she felt anxious about leaving. The dog easily picked up on her emotions and started licking her hands. She wrapped her arms around the dog and fell asleep deeply.

When she woke up, Sugar was chewing on a blanket. "You must be hungry, my little buddy," said Daisy yawning and got out of the bed. She pulled her hair up into a messy bun and walked to the kitchen.

Robert was having his breakfast. Daisy filled the dog's bowel with kibble, but Sugar didn't touch his food. He settled down at Robert's feet, hoping to get a piece of omelette. The dog was dripping saliva from his mouth. Robert got annoyed and gestured for him to go. "Eat your food," he said in a stern voice.

Daisy added a little cottage cheese to the dog's usual food. The trick worked; she made the picky dog eat his food. Daisy perched on a stool beside her father. "I have something very important I need to tell you." She said.

Robert continued eating in silence.

"I'm getting married, Dad," she said in one breath.

Robert rolled his eyes at her in sarcastic disbelief. "What a big rush."

"Why are you against my marriage?" Daisy raised her voice.

"Huh! What an absurd thing to get married after a few dates. You don't even know him."

Daisy didn't like a note of irony in his voice. "There is no timeline for falling in love and getting married. If you care for me a little bit, please respect my decision," she said, convincingly.

Robert wiped his mouth with a napkin. "Who knows, maybe he is a psychopath straight out of a horror movie. I smell something fishy about him. Isn't it weird that he wants to get married so fast?" His face flushed red.

"I'm tired of your biting comments. It seems to me you don't want to see me happy," she sighed heavily. "Dad, you taught me how to walk and you let go of my hands so quickly. Why did you distance yourself from me? You never said to me: 'I love you,' you never hugged me as a child." Daisy sobbed, unable to control her emotions. Her eyes were brimming with tears.

Robert smashed his fist down on the table as anger seized him. The loud noise startled the dog. He lunged forward and quickly ran out of the kitchen.

"I thought you were grateful that I raised you by myself. I did my best to give you a good life," Robert let out an exasperated sigh through his nose, trying his best not to yell. "I see you are as stubborn as your mother," he said and took his wedding ring off. Robert rubbed his finger nervously. "Wearing this ring for so many years left ugly stains around my finger," he said and handed his gold wedding ring to his daughter. "Give it to him on your wedding day," he added through gritted teeth.

As he walked out of the kitchen, she felt lonely. The feeling was so strong she burst into tears. Daisy desperately needed a hug from a mother whom she had never met. She craved her mother's love and care. She wanted to hear her say 'Everything will be fine' she sighed deeply with sorrow. Releasing emotions stuck in her body, she wiped her tears with a paper tissue. Her thoughts were interrupted by a phone call.

"Good morning, my love. I have fantastic news! We are getting married at a registry office next Saturday. Everything is arranged for the ceremony." Said Eddie with excitement.

Daisy got puzzled. After a moment's hesitation, she said: "Oh, I really didn't expect it to happen so soon."

"Me neither. I guess luck is on our side." He replied.

"I have so many things to get done." She murmured.

"Don't worry, dear. There is nothing you can't handle. My phone battery is pretty low, I've got to go now."

"Have a nice day," she said after a pause.

Daisy applied concealer to cover up her puffy eyes. She quickly got dressed and made her way to the office.

The secretary was watering the little cactus with a spray bottle. Daisy approached her, smiling. "I see your cactus has grown from short and fat to thin and tall," she said, giggling.

"I talk to my plant every day; I think it helped my prickly friend to grow faster."

Daisy smiled broadly. "Is Ms. Brown in her office?" She asked.

The secretary nodded her head.

Daisy walked along the corridor. When she approached the office of the editor -in chief, the sweat laid on her face. It felt clammy and cool on her skin. Ms. Brown looked at her sharply over the top of the newspaper. "Did you need anything?" She asked.

Daisy nodded yes and took a step forward. "Ms. Brown, I wanted to personally inform you that I'm getting married in a few days. I'm planning to go on a honeymoon trip soon," she said. Her mouth felt dry and sticky as there was no saliva in it.

Ms. Brown gulped down her tea. "You know the general rule of our contract. Unfortunately, you need to leave the company as you prioritized your personal life over work." She said in a strict voice.

Daisy's face turned pale. She looked down in embarrassment. Ms. Brown turned over the page of the newspaper. "If you think that marriage will change your life for better, I won't stop you." She said.

Daisy struggled holding back her tears. "Ms. Brown, it was an honour working for your publishing company," she said and walked towards the door. Daisy was lifting and settling down each foot very slowly, hoping that she would stop her, but Ms. Brown didn't even bother to change her mind.

Daisy leaned back against the wall in the narrow corridor and wept bitterly. After a brief pause, she walked towards her room with heavy steps.

"What happened, honey. Are you okay?" Leo asked with deep concern in his eyes.

"I just got fired," said Daisy, still sobbing.

"Are you kidding me?!" Grace exclaimed, wide-eyed. "You are so good at writing; our boss will never let you go."

"When I told Ms. Brown that I was going to get married, she asked me to leave the company," said Daisy with a sigh.

"Wait a minute, are you getting married?"

"Yes."

"When?"

"Next Saturday."

Leo chuckled lightly. "You are crazy, girl." He gave her a poke in the arm.

Daisy scrunched up her eyes and smiled softly. " Guys, you are my best friends; I want you to be my witnesses at the wedding ceremony."

Grace clapped her hands in excitement. "We would be more than happy to support you."

Leo turned his joyful eyes to Daisy. "By the way, do you have a bridal gown?" He asked.

"I will be wearing a simple dress as we aren't going to have a big wedding," she said, pulling the inner corners of her eyebrows up and together.

"No matter how big or small you wedding is, it's your special day and you have to be dressed to kill. Just trust me on that. I will take you to the best wedding dress designer. She will help us choose the perfect gown for you."

Daisy gave her friends a bear hug. Her cheeks turned pink as her mood lifted instantly. She totally forgot that she just lost her job.

Chapter Five

The day Daisy was waiting for her entire life has arrived. The bride felt all jittery before taking the final plunge. She found herself second guessing her decision to get married so soon. Her knees were shaking with nervousness. She felt as if she were in a different reality decked out in a wedding gown and surrounded by her friends.

"Are you ready?" Leo asked her. He kept watching on her dress and veil to make sure it looked great.

Daisy squeezed her eyes shut.

"Take a deep breath, relax. Everything will go well," he said and picked up the bride's train to put the crystal wedding shoes on her.

"Oh, these shoes are too tight for me," said Daisy with a concern in her voice.

"Honey, you just have to simply wear them anyway and suffer in the name of fashion for a few hours," Leo replied convincingly.

Daisy gave him a smile of approval. Grace handed her a wedding bouquet. The bunch of white roses grouped together were tied with a pink ribbon. Daisy looked at herself in a mirror. She knew she looked good in her mermaid wedding dress. It fitted her perfectly on her body, creating the illusion of a wasplike figure. The attention-grabbing silhouette gave her a wow factor.

A few minutes later, Eddie poked his head in the room, but Leo quickly blocked his way. "It's a bad luck for the groom to see the bride in a wedding gown before the ceremony. You are only allowed to meet at the altar," he said and locked the door.

Grace touched up Daisy's lipstick. She applied a coat of matte lip balm on her lips. "You are the most beautiful bride in the world! Eddie is one lucky guy." She exclaimed.

Daisy leaned over and kissed her. She left a lipstick stain on her chubby cheek.

Entering the registry office, Daisy felt her breath rising and falling fast. Eddie gave her a large smile. He was wearing a navy suit and a boutonniere with a white rose. The groom took the bride's hand and squeezed it tightly. Daisy bent forward and whispered in his ear. "I'm a little bit nervous."

"Don't be scared, I'm with you," he said, caressing her palm.

The registrar made a short statement about marriage. Daisy felt hot and sweaty. Her heart was pounding faster and her vision got darker. At the back of her mind she was bothered about what would happen post marriage. She took a deep breath in attempt to calm herself down. Leo sensed her nervousness. He rubbed his hand in slow circles on her back, trying to console her.

When the exchange of wedding rings began, Eddie kissed the bride's hand. "Today is the beginning of the rest of our lives. I vow to love you always. I give you this simple gold ring as a symbol of my eternal love for you," his voice boomed loudly. He placed the wedding ring on the fourth finger on her left hand.

In that very moment Daisy first felt like an adult. She felt more self-confident and less insecure. "I will take your love, Eddie to give me joy and make me a better person. I promise to be there with you when you need me. I vow to love you and honour you," she said, looking deeply into his eyes. Placing the bouquet on the table, she put her father's thick gold ring on Eddie's finger.

The registrar asked the witnesses to sign the certificate of marriage. Eddie handed the document to Mr. Irving. The veteran soldier was dressed in his military uniform. He had a proud smile on his face, it seemed that his whole mind and body were smiling. He was sitting up straighter in his wheelchair. Daisy gave him a smile, showing appreciation. "Thank you, Mr. Irving, for your support."

"I wish your uncle were here."

"I believe he is watching over me."

"Of course, dear. He must be very proud of you." He said and grinned.

"You are so kind to me." Replied Daisy.

Mrs. Irving pulled the small jewellery box out of her purse and handed it to Daisy. "This is a wedding gift to you, a pair of pearl earrings." She said.

Daisy was amazed by the gift. "Thank you so much, Mrs. Irving. How did you know I always wanted to have pearl earrings?" She exclaimed and immediately inserted the earrings in her earlobes.

Mrs. Irving looked pleased. She smiled broadly, showing her teeth.

The wedding ceremony lasted about twenty minutes. Despite the fact that only four witnesses attended the ceremony, Daisy didn't forget the bouquet toss tradition. She threw her wedding bouquet over her shoulder to be caught by Grace as she wanted to pass on her good fortune to her friend, but in a blink of an eye, Leo caught the bride's bouquet. "Oh, my God! I will be the next to get married," He exclaimed.

Daisy gave a belly laugh. Leo laughed with her. He pulled his phone out of his pocket." Let's take a good selfie photo," he turned the front camera on.

"Please be quick. We are going to be late to catch a flight," said Eddie and smiled for the picture.

Daisy twirled around in her dress. "I'm going to get changed now. I will be right back," she said and went to the restroom. Leo followed her to help carry her dress up the stairs. She put on her jeans and a white shirt and handed her bridal gown to Leo. "Thanks for making me feel like a queen on my special day."

"You deserve all the best, honey."

The newly married couple sat in the cab. Leo put Daisy's luggage in the trunk and poked his head inside the car window. "Have a blast on your honeymoon!" He exclaimed.

Daisy blew a kiss to her friends. They waved back.

***

Finally, the couple could have their much-anticipated honeymoon. After a long -haul flight they have landed on the island of Hawaii.

"It's time to unwind and begin the new chapter together," Eddie stretched his arms wide apart.

"Let's forget the world and just enjoy each other," replied Daisy, softly kissing his upper lip. She inhaled the humid air infused with salt. The sun's rays were much stronger what she had experienced at home.

They took the shuttle bus to the resort. The bright pink and happy yellow colours of frangipani flowers caught Daisy's eye. Friendly front desk associates welcomed just married couple in with open arms. They put a wreath of flowers around Daisy's neck as a token of blessing.

"Aloha!" Daisy greeted them with a big smile.

The scent of frangipani flowers floated on the breeze. The rustic honeymoon cottage with ocean view immediately put Daisy into a state of aloha. She was thrilled to see the kissing towel swans and heart shaped rose petals on the king-size bed. "How romantic!" She exclaimed.

Eddie gave a snorting giggle. Tossing the towels over the chair, he threw himself on the bed.

"Oh, I wanted to take a photo of kissing swan towels," she said, pursing her lips to the side.

"Come lay with me, dear," he said, yawning.

"I will unpack our bags and will join you." She replied.

Daisy unpacked all the clothes she needed and left the rest in the suitcase. She got dolled up in white lace lingerie which her friend, Grace gifted her on her wedding day. Her nipples were visible through the non-padded lace bra. She put on a cute sheer nightgown as she wanted to play a little striptease to evoke Eddie's fantasies.

When she came out of the bathroom, Eddie was already sound asleep. He was snoring loudly, giving a rattling sound through his mouth. Staring down at him, Daisy let out a deep sigh and put a blanket over him. She quietly opened the balcony door and walked out.

The sun was about to set. Its bloody red colour began to spread all over the sky. Catching the unexpected sunset put her into piece of mind. She forgot everything for a moment, just admired the view of nature. She let her imagination run free. She fantasized about dreaming of a life in a cosy house, playing on a beach with her future child, writing her first novel about motherhood.... Even thinking about it all made her feel satisfied and happy.

Eddie woke her up with a kiss the next morning. "You look like an angel when you sleep," he said and wrapped her up in his arms.

Daisy smiled; her shyness was rather endearing. Eddie kissed her neck and shoulders; his scruffy beard tickled her skin. It felt like small sharp needles. She lightly scratched her skin.

"Sweetheart, I'm so sorry that I spoiled our first night. I just had travel fatigue and fell asleep like a log with my clothes on," he said apologetically.

"Well, I'm giving you another chance," she said and threw the blanket off in an attempt to turn him on. She gave him a prolonged deep eye contact. Unbuttoning his shirt, she slowly slid her hands onto his hairy chest. Her tender touch drew him like a magnet. He leaned forward and pressed his lips to hers. "You are so sexy," he whispered in her ear.

Her whole body woke up with energy. Eddie took off his shirt in one quick movement. Taking her earlobe between his lips, he began tugging it gently. He unhooked her bra and licked her pear-shaped breasts. He moved his tongue around her nipples in a slow circular motion. Eddie noticed that she was trembling. "Don't be scared," he groaned. His pupils were dilated. He squeezed her breasts with his rough callously hands and sucked them deeply. Her nipples were hard like rubber. She moaned with pleasure. She felt his full weight pressing against her body. The room was filled with strong arousal and heavy breathing. He pulled his pants down along with his boxers. Daisy stared at his small pink sausage. It was the size of her little finger. It startled her, but she didn't want to hurt her partner's self-esteem. Her eyes drifted upward to his chest. She nibbled his nipples gently. It tickled his sensory nerve endings and made him go week in his knees. Eddie put her on top of him as he wanted to build sexual trust and intimacy with her.

Daisy felt pain after penetration, but forced herself not to fight against it. He ejaculated very quickly. His body was covered with sweat. His face was red. It seemed he was embarrassed about finishing too soon. Daisy was silent. She could feel her heartbeat speed up. Eddie pulled her against his chest. "Did it feel good?" He asked her.

Daisy nodded and forced herself a tight-lipped smile. Eddie caressed her cheek gently. "I'm starving, let's go eat breakfast," he said and got out of bed.

"I'll take a quick shower, just give me five minutes." She replied.

"Take your time, sweetheart. I'll go to the buffet restaurant and get a nice table for us," he said and put on his polo shirt and shorts. He quickly brushed his teeth and pecked her on the cheek.

As soon as he walked out of the room, she removed the bed sheets stained with blood. She rubbed the soap into the stain area of the sheet and scrubbed it by hand in the water. Once the stain got invisible, she dried it with a hairdryer. Daisy felt emotionally exhausted when she stepped into the shower. Hot water gave her an instant relief. She put on her leopard print beaded kaftan over the black swimsuit and went to the restaurant.

Eddie was sitting at an outdoor table overlooking the beach. The table was flooded with dishes. He was eating a soft-boiled egg in an egg cup with buttery toast. Daisy took a sit in front of him. "Enjoy your meal," she said and poured herself a glass of watermelon juice.

"Try Hawaiian sweet rolls. There is nothing better than a warm roll with butter and strawberry jam," he said as he took a sip of tea.

"I will start my breakfast with yogurt," replied Daisy. She opened the plastic yogurt container and sprinkled the handful of fresh blueberries on top of the plain yogurt.

The sun gently fell on her skin. Daisy shielded her eyes with her sunglasses. "Let's quickly finish breakfast and hit the beach until the sun is over our head." She said.

Eddie ate his poached chicken sandwich in about three bites. "I'm ready, sweetheart," he quickly stood up from his seat.

The inviting beach with aqua blue water, tall palm trees, and silky white sand made Daisy feel lighter. She kicked off her sandals and ran along the beach with her arms wide open. She felt as if her arms were turned into wings and she were flying high in the sky. Her silky hair flew out after her like a mane of a horse. She turned her head and waved at her husband, inviting him to follow her. Eddie stood leaning against the coconut palm tree. "I'd rather sit in a shade," he responded, smiling.

The sun's rays were shimmering on the balmy waves. Daisy slipped off her kaftan and threw it on the sand. She dipped her toes into the water. It was so cold she got goosebumps on her skin. She curled her toes and gently splashed herself with water to avoid cold water shock. After a moment's hesitation, she took a dip. Daisy lay on her back and gazed up at the sky. She fluttered her legs while circling her arms in a windmill motion. She felt as if she were floating on a fluffy white cloud.

Eddie noticed two wooden beach beds with blue striped matrasses and umbrellas from a distance. He positioned the umbrella so that he could rest in the shade. He quickly took off his clothes. His skin was white like white wool. He lay down on the beach bed and watched a yellow parachute fly overhead. When the sun's rays started biting into him, he quickly got up and stepped into the ocean very carefully to acclimatize his body to cold water. "Grr! It's freezing!" He exclaimed, annoyed.

Daisy splashed the water on his body and face, giggling without a care. Eddie covered his face with his hands. "Stop it! Have you lost your mind?" He yelled. His voice sounded like thunder. It was so loud that it made her ears hurt.

"Sorry," she said and without looking at him marched to the beach bed.

Eddie followed her with quick steps. "Sweetheart, I didn't mean to upset you. Please, don't be mad at me," he said and gently kissed her on the cheek.

Daisy gave him a slight, asymmetric smile. The left side of her mouth was little bit higher than the right side. She made herself comfortable on the wooden bed, hoping to get a golden tan. She closed her eyes and inhaled deeply. The sound of the slow crushing waves comforted her. It gave her a sense of calmness and almost lulled her to sleep. Her serenity was disturbed by her husband's moan and fretful complaint.

"What's the matter with you?" Daisy asked.

"I got badly sunburned." He sighed.

Daisy leaned forward and saw red spots on his shoulders and chest. "Oh, poor you! Your shoulders resemble cherry popsicles," She exclaimed as she touched his arm.

"Ouch! That hurts," he whined. "I need to stay out of the sun and apply a cool compress to heal the skin."

"Sure, let's quickly get out of here," she said and slipped into her kaftan in a blink of an eye.

Eddie buttoned up his shirt to protect his skin from the sun. When the material of the shirt touched his skin, he felt like he was stabbed with tiny needless.

As soon as he entered the room, he opened his first aid kit. Luckily, a small box contained all the items he needed. He applied cool gauze padding to the burnt area. Rubbing a thin layer of antibiotic ointment on the skin caused him to squeeze his eyes shut against the unbearable pain. Daisy was torn by guilt. "It's my fault that you got a sunburn. I wanted to stay longer on the beach," she said with genuine concern.

"It's okay, sweetheart. I will stay indoors during midday when the sun is at its peak in the sky," he said and zipped the small green box shut. "Hey, let's have lunch," Eddie nudged her lightly with his knee.

Daisy nodded her head in approval and put the room key in her purse.

There was a long queue of diners at a buffet restaurant. Everyone was trying to sneak up to the counter as they wanted to get in first. While standing in a queue, Daisy was deciding what to eat. "My stomach is growling from hunger,' she said, giggling.

"It means your brain is trying to send a message to your digestive organs that it's time to eat," he said and pinched her nose.

When their turn came, Daisy couldn't resist the urge to pop some olives into her mouth. A fresh island fish wrapped in a taro leaf looked mouth-watering. She held her plate close to the serving dish to avoid spillage. Eddie loaded his plate with two scoops of brown rice, macaroni salad and fried chicken.

Daisy took a bite of the exotic dish. The fish juice was soaked into taro leaves. "It's so flavourful and juicy each bite leaves me hungrier for more."

"Let me try your dish," said Eddie and stuck his fork in it. "Mm! He exclaimed, expressing pleasure. "Actually, I prefer taro leaves more than fish."

When their bellies were satisfyingly full, they walked towards the front door, linking arms. The buffet counter stuff member stopped them with a wave of his hand. "Excuse me, you forgot to pay for the meal."

Eddie paused for a moment. A vertical wrinkle appeared between his eyebrows. "I thought my holiday package included three meals a day," his voice got a little raspy as he made a lame excuse.

"No, sir. Your package includes just breakfast for two."

"Oh, I'm sorry for a misunderstanding," said Eddie and pulled the credit card out of his wallet.

He paid the dining bill and sighed, shrugging his shoulders. Daisy broke the awkward silence with a question. "Eddie, what would you say if we visit the tropical rainforest today?"

"As you wish, sweetheart." He replied.

While the sun was shining brightly, the gentle raindrops began to fall to the ground. Daisy started jumping up and down. "Sun-shower!" She cried out loud in childish excitement.

Eddie cast a wry glance in her direction, turning the corners of his mouth downwards. "I'm afraid we have to postpone a trip to the rainforest. Rain isn't my favourite weather."

Daisy exhaled noisily through her pursed lips. "Whatever! Let's sit under the shade of a tree, at least we'll get a breath of fresh air."

Eddie mimicked her facial expression and pedantic voice as well as breathing pattern. Daisy stuck her tongue out at him as an expression of taunting.

They sat on a wooden bench under the leaning branches of a tree. Neither of them smiled. The small yellow birds were chirping and hopping from branch to branch. It seemed a little rain didn't worry them at all. Daisy noticed a young couple standing in the rain, kissing and hugging each other.

They didn't care a whit if the whole world was watching them. Daisy felt a sudden pity for herself. She realised that her honeymoon wasn't as romantic and special as she expected.

After a long, breathless pause Eddie said sharply: "I need to take a cold shower and calm my sunburned skin. Would you come with me?"

"I'd like to stay here for a little while, if you don't mind," she replied and gave him the room key.

"Sure, I don't mind at all," Eddie jumped over the water puddle and headed to the cottage.

Daisy let out a long sigh of sadness. Her gaze drifted again to the young couple kissing each other. The man swept his partner in his arms and spun her around. The woman started laughing loudly. Her hearty laughter was so contagious that it made Daisy laugh to herself.

Meanwhile, the rain has stopped. Daisy was about to take a stroll along the beach when she heard her cell phone ringing in her purse. She was nicely surprised to hear Mr. Irving's voice. "Hello, Daisy. I hope it's not a bad time for me to call." He said.

"I'm happy to hear from you, Mr. Irving," she replied in a quivering voice.

"But why is your voice shaky? Is your husband behaving well?"

After a moment's hesitation, she said: "Yes."

"Are you really happy, dear?"

"I find it strange that I don't know if I'm happy or not."

"You can't be half happy, dear. You should share your feelings with your husband. It will help you to have an emotionally fulfilling relationship."

"Thank you, Mr. Irving for your understanding."

"Take care of yourself. I want to see a big smile on your face."

Daisy chuckled lightly. She tucked her phone into her pocket and ran to the cottage with quick steps.

Eddie was sitting on the coach watching TV. Daisy sat next to him and put her head on his shoulder. "I missed you,' she whispered in his ear.

"Me too, sweetheart," he said without taking his eyes off the TV.

Daisy turned the TV off and kissed him gently on the neck. Eddie let out a little smile. He grabbed the remote control from her and turned the TV back on. Daisy leaned towards him. "To be honest I feel a bit distant from you," she said and looked into his eyes.

Eddie caressed the top of her head. He gently stroked her silky and smooth hair with his fingertips. "Don't be silly, sweetheart. You are the most important person in my life."

Daisy gave him a tight hug to let him know how much she was happy to hear it. Eddie slightly pushed her away by putting both hands on her chest. "Sweetheart, my shoulders are still sore from sunburn."

"Sorry, I forgot about it."

"I'd like to watch a football game tonight. Would you mind if I skip dinner? Besides, I'm not hungry at all."

"No problem, I'm not hungry either," she replied and went to the balcony.

The night was slowly coming. Daisy gazed up at the dark blue sky and noticed a tiny star twinkling with light. She had a feeling the star was sparkling brightly just for her. "Hello, Mother!" She exclaimed. Her large brown eyes lit up with delight. "I believe you turned into a bright star to watch me from above." She sighed.

In a blink of an eye, the star's brightness increased. It seemed to her that the star began growing in size. Gazing at the star replaced her worry and fear with hope. Her mind started to vent. She had a feeling the sky was listening to her. She blew a kiss to the shining star and walked into the room.

Eddie has fallen asleep with the TV on. Daisy switched the TV off and slipped into bed. She carefully rolled to the left side, avoiding touching his sunburned shoulders.

In the morning Daisy woke up in the same exact body position as when she fell asleep. Her neck felt tight and tense. It was very uncomfortable to move it from side to side. Eddie wiped the sleep crust out of his eyes with his fingers. "Sweetheart, let me give you a little neck massage. It will relieve the tension," he said as he sat up in bed.

"Thanks, that would be great." She replied.

Eddie placed his partner in a comfortable seated position. He gave her a caring touch as an invitation to relax. He used long, gentle strokes along the surface of her neck muscles. Finding tension knots, he applied focused pressure and made circular motion with his thumbs.

"Oh, I feel so much better," she said with a moan.

Eddie grinned. "Hey, a bright idea came to my mind. What if we take extra food from the breakfast buffet and make packed lunch? It would be so much fun eating at the beach." Excitement was obvious in his voice.

Daisy rolled her eyes up and to the right, thinking about his suggestion. She knew it was unethical to take food home from the breakfast buffet, but she didn't want to let her husband down. She just loved the naughtiness in his eyes. "Why not?!" She exclaimed.

He leapt out of bed and quickly got dressed.

Daisy and Eddie arrived first at the buffet restaurant. Eddie wondered over to the long table full of various dishes. Daisy lingered near the fruit salads. "I'm never hungry when I wake up," she said as she filled the plate with colourful grapes and a slice of watermelon.

"Breakfast is the most important meal of a day, sweetheart. It provides you with energy to get through the morning," he replied and poured some honey over his hot porridge. He plunged into his food and ate until he was full. "Can you hand me a plastic bag?" He asked her and took a sip of milk.

Daisy started laughing loudly. "You have a milk moustache above your upper lip," she said, still laughing.

Eddie laughed with her and wiped his mouth with his serviette. He neatly wrapped some sandwiches and biscuits in white paper napkins and put them in a plastic bag. Daisy picked mini yogurts and fluffy croissant rolls and placed them in the beach bag.

Walking out of the Buffett restaurant they raised their arms and hit open hands together cheerfully.

"I would like to experience swimming with dolphins and fulfil my childhood dream," said Daisy with pure excitement.

"That's awesome. You should definitely do that. I'd better stay at home to avoid the sun," he replied and kissed her on the forehead.

Daisy boarded a shuttle bus to the dolphin park. All she was thinking was what dolphin's skin would feel like. As she approached the pool, she felt a rush of adrenaline in her body. Her heart started beating faster than normal. She got in the pool and touched the top of the head of the medium sized dolphin. Its skin was smooth and felt rubbery. Daisy noticed lots of tiny scars and scratches on the dolphin's nose. The curious creature looked deeply into her eyes. It seemed the dolphin was trying to read out her thoughts. "I have been waiting to meet you for a very long time!" Exclaimed Daisy and chuckled softly. The dolphin grinned at her, showing equal sized conical shaped teeth and made a loud whistling sound as if somehow trying to tell her something. The adorable dolphin began game by throwing the ball towards Daisy. She quickly caught a ball. Her belly shook with joyful laughter. Daisy and her new friend tossed the red ball back and forth for several times. Daisy laughed so hard her core muscles became sore. The harmony between them was disturbed by the dolphin trainer's high-pitched voice. "Your time is up!" He said to Daisy and gestured for her to come out of the water.

Daisy's brow furrowed. "Can I take a picture with the dolphin?" She asked the trainer.

"Sure, but please be quick." He replied.

Daisy gently touched the dolphin's face and gave it a farewell kiss on the mouth. The photographer captured the magical moment on the camera.

When Daisy got home, she told Eddie about her adventure and showed him a picture with the dolphin. Her eyes were gleaming with joy. She had smile lines around her mouth.

"I'm glad you had a great time, sweetheart. I bet you are hungry now," said Eddie and opened the mini bar refrigerator. He pulled a napkin-wrapped sandwich out of the fridge and handed it to her. "Enjoy your lunch, my partner in crime," he winked at her.

Daisy ate the sandwich in one bite, accompanied by a strawberry yogurt. "My lunch was delicious," she said, giggling.

Every muscle in his face smiled. "My plan to take food home from a buffet was brilliant. We have freedom to eat whenever we like," he said with his chin up high.

Eddie's plan worked just fine until the last day of their vacation arrived. Daisy packed up her suitcase, placing the clothes she would need first at the top. Then she started rolling her husband's clothes, but Eddie didn't let her put his belongings in his bag. " Sweetheart, It's breakfast time. If we don't go to the buffet now there will be no food left for us," he said and put the folded plastic bag in his pocket.

"Okay, I will pack your bag later," she replied and followed him out of the cottage. She deeply inhaled fresh air. It filled her lungs and made her more energized and alive.

They entered the buffet restaurant and sat at their usual table overlooking the ocean. Daisy glanced towards the shore with her eyes half closed, not paying attention to anything around her. "I'd like to do fun things on the last day of our vacation," she said with a bright smile on her face.

"Sure, sweetheart," replied Eddie and put the napkin -wrapped sandwiches in a plastic bag.

"I feel thirsty. I will go and grab some juice while you finish your breakfast," said Daisy and went towards the sideboard table. She poured freshly squeezed orange juice into the glass and took a sip. Turning around she saw the buffet counter staff member talking to Eddie, his brows were furrowed with concern. Eddie was shrugging his shoulders in disbelief. Daisy looked at them wide-eyed, wondering what could have happened in the moment she went to get orange juice. As she approached her husband, she was met with his implacable expression. His eyes were almost jumping out of their sockets.

"What happened?" She asked.

Eddie shook his head. "How Ironic!" He exclaimed. "I'm not allowed to take my leftovers home from the breakfast buffet. Who would have thought that such a shameful thing could happen?" He scowled.

The buffet counter stuff member wiped sweat from his forehead with a tissue. "Sir, I'm sorry, but you aren't allowed to take more than you can consume away from a hotel buffet," his face turned red when he spoke.

Eddie put the plastic bag filled with food on the table and walked out of the restaurant without looking back. Daisy followed him with quick steps. "Please, don't let this incident ruin our day," she said to him with pleading eyes.

Eddie kept quiet. He was breathing heavily, flaring his nostrils out. Entering the cottage, he threw himself backwards on the bed. Daisy lay down next to him. "Are you sad?" She asked as she caressed his cheek softly.

"I'm fine," he replied and lifted her hair from her neck. "I'd like to get some sleep, sweetheart. As soon as we arrive in Sydney I have to go to the clinic. I'm working a night shift tomorrow. I kind of miss my job."

"Fair enough, I won't disturb you," she said and quickly got up. She pulled the window blinds down to block the bright sunlight.

Eddie gave a huge yawn. "Sweetheart, what is your work schedule?" He asked.

Daisy turned pale. "Unfortunately, my boss fired me as I broke the contract rules and got married."

Eddie jumped out of bed. "Are you kidding me?"

"I'm serious."

"What are you going to do?"

"I'm planning to write a novel."

Eddie raised his eyebrows at her and gave a nervous chuckle which was provoked by the expression of alarm.

"What are you laughing at?" Daisy asked, annoyed.

"Do you really believe that people still read books nowadays?" He cackled with malicious glee, showing his peg shaped teeth. His laughter was so cold and unpleasant it pushed her away.

Daisy looked straight into his eyes. "I thought you were a non-materialistic person with spiritual and intellectual values," she said with a sigh.

"Save your romantic fantasies for your novel," said Eddie in a sarcastic tone.

Daisy was emotionally numb. She felt as though Eddie had a remote control in his hands and was continuously switching channels without asking her what she wanted to watch. She bit her tongue to stop herself from crying. Eddie poured himself a glass of water. "I thought you were a successful journalist. How can I tell my parents that I married a loser?"

His cruel words stabbed through her heart like an arrow. Daisy was so disgusted at his behaviour that she almost fainted. She stumbled over a table leg and landed on the carpet.

Eddie gave her his hand to help her to get up off the floor, but Daisy pushed his hand away. "Take your stuff and get out of here!" She yelled. "I'm not willing to be your wife anymore," she found it hard to keep her tone low.

"I don't care," he said, showing no emotion. Eddie didn't even blink an eye. It took him less than a minute to pack his bag.

"You are a greedy pig!" She exclaimed in rage.

Eddie slammed the door shut. Daisy let out an audible gasp and started crying like a child. "Oh, God, what did I do to deserve this?" Her voice was soaked with tears. She swallowed a lump in her throat and blinked away her hot tears. She grabbed the phone and called the front desk receptionist to get a cab for her to the airport. With trembling hands, she collected her luggage and went to the lobby. Eddie was sitting on the sofa and munching nuts. She made an eye contact with him to make him feel embarrassed, but he quickly averted her gaze.

The cab arrived at six o'clock sharp. Daisy thanked the hotel concierge for the hospitality and walked out the front door. In a blink of an eye, Eddie jumped into a cab and was whisked away. Daisy was perplexed, unable to move. She put the suitcase down on the pavement. Her heart was heavier than her luggage. It was the moment she felt abandoned.

"Ma'am, did you book a taxi to the airport?" The driver's voice brought her out of her unpleasant thoughts.

Daisy nodded yes and got into the car. The driver was listening to Hawaiian folk songs. He was moving his head up and down to the rhythm of the beat. "Ma'am, did you enjoy your vacation?" He asked.

Daisy didn't reply. She stared at her wedding ring with cold eyes. She felt angry with herself for letting her husband emotionally manipulate her. Looking at the ring felt like a slap in the face. She wanted so much to get rid of the memories. She pulled the wedding ring off her finger and threw it out of the car window. Poking her head out, she let the breeze ruffle her hair.

When she got on an airplane, she felt sharp pain in the back of her head. Deep down, she was relieved that physical pain has distracted her brain temporarily from emotional distress.

From the corner of her eye, she spotted Eddie sitting comfortably in the aisle seat. Daisy asked the fellow passenger if he could switch seats with her as she didn't want to sit next to Eddie. She gave him a begging look; her head was slightly tilted down and her eyes were looking up. She seemed so desperate, the fellow passenger couldn't ignore her pleading and agreed to swap seats with her. Daisy settled into the aisle seat behind Eddie. The cabin crew started preparing the airplane for take-off. She curled into a ball and fastened her seat belt. Her mind was occupied by one thought -what to say to her father. She struggled to find an explanation for why her marriage failed.

Chapter Six

The plane landed safely in Sydney. Everyone was eager to get out of the cramped tube and get back into the world. When the seat belt sign turned off the passengers immediately stood up from their seats. Daisy wanted to stay longer on the plane. She let others go ahead of her as she didn't want to bump into her husband. Eddie rushed towards the exit in order to get off the plane first. Daisy pulled her bag out of the overhead compartment and slowly wheeled it out of the plane.

It was nearly midnight. Daisy went to the taxi stand which had a long queue of cars lined up. She got into the first taxi in line. Pulling the cell phone out of her bag, she dialled her friend's number. "Hello, Grace. I hope I didn't wake you up," her voice sounded choked even to her own ears.

Grace sensed that something was wrong. "Daisy, I missed you so much. Where are you?"

"I've just arrived. Can I spend a night at your place?"

"Sure, is everything alright?"

"I'll tell you when I see you," she said and ended the conversation before tears produced by glands around her eyes.

When Daisy told the taxi driver her destination, he groaned. "If you told me earlier that your trip was so short, I wouldn't have taken you. I've been waiting in the queue for hours." He complained.

"How much do I owe you?" She asked.

"Twenty-five dollars," he replied and looked at her in the rear-view mirror.

"I understand your annoyance. I can give you thirty dollars, that's all I have."

"Okay," he shook his head.

Daisy rolled the car window down and took a sharp breath. As the taxi approached Grace's apartment building, she saw her friend standing on the balcony, waving at her.

Grace welcomed her with open arms. She noticed that Daisy no longer wore her wedding ring. "How are you, dear?" She asked.

"I broke up with Eddie," replied Daisy, her bottom lip started quivering.

"Oh, I'm so sorry. Please don't worry, it's normal for a newly married couple to argue."

Daisy started crying. Her tears were flowing quickly, blurring her vision. "My honeymoon was the worst experience of my life. I had a feeling that I jumped off a cliff into the ocean without knowing how to swim. I kept flapping my hands to keep my head above water. I felt so tired I died inside," she said, still crying. She poured out her heart to her friend. Daisy knew she would listen to her without judgement. Grace allowed her to feel heard and valued. She has perfectly fit the role of a counsellor listening attentively to a depressed patient during a conversation. She made mint tea for her. "It will sooth your body and calm you mind," she said and handed her a cup of tea.

"Who would have thought that my marriage would end so quickly?!" Daisy sighed.

"It's hard to believe that Eddie turned out to be such a douchebag. I really thought your love story would stand the test of time, " said Grace and shook her head in annoyance.

"Eddie is like a balloon, if you pop it, you will see that there is nothing inside." Daisy blew on her tea to cool it faster.

"I feel so bad that your honeymoon wasn't what you expected."

"At least I had one pleasant moment," said Daisy and wiped the tears from her cheeks.

"And what was that about?" Grace asked.

"Playing fetch with a dolphin," she said and chuckled softly at the thought.

The next morning when Daisy woke up, her friend was already gone. She found a letter on the bedside table, saying: 'Good morning, D. I'm off to work. I made fluffy double chocolate pancakes for you. I hope your day goes well. Love you, Grace.'

Daisy dressed quickly and made her way to the kitchen. She didn't touch the food as she had a loss of appetite. She poured herself a cup of black coffee and strolled to the window. She wasn't ready to face her father. Her mind was racing with repetitive thoughts and she couldn't think straight. Daisy took a long sip of her coffee. She picked up her cell phone and dialled Mr. Irving's number.

"Good morning, Mr. Irving. Do you have a minute to talk?" She asked.

"I'm always at your service, dear."

"I don't feel well. Every second I spent with Eddie made me feel physically and emotionally drained. I decided to get a divorce to end this miserable relationship."

"I'm sincerely sorry to hear that. If you really think that you are unhappy with your partner, don't let him steal your vulnerable time. Remind yourself that you have a bright future ahead. Trust me dear, day by day you will start moving on. You need to survive the pain by building resilience."

"I'm afraid to face my father. He warned me not to rush into marriage, but I didn't listen to him."

"You don't have to feel ashamed. Tell him the truth and take the burden off your shoulders."

"Thank you so much for encouraging me, Mr. Irving."

"Call me anytime just if you need someone to talk to."

"I appreciate your concern," she said. Her voice sounded more energized.

Daisy gazed up at the sky. She couldn't see the sun; the sky was full of granite grey clouds. She felt as dull as the weather. Walking up the stairs to her apartment, she heard her dog bark. It seemed the dog sensed that she was close. Daisy rang the doorbell; her palms grew sweaty as she was nervous. Robert opened the door. His face was covered by shaving foam. "Long time no see," he said to her and poked his head around the door. "Where is your husband?" He beckoned her inside.

Daisy turned even paler. "I broke up with him," she murmured without looking at her father and wheeled her small suitcase into the hallway.

"Huh! He exclaimed. "It's not surprising that your marriage was over in a blink of an eye," he said and rubbed the towel against his face.

A single drop of sorrow fell from the corner of her eye. Daisy felt embarrassed and ashamed of her failure. For a moment Robert felt sympathy for her. He wiped her tear away with his thumb. "I know you are suffering now, but believe me, nothing is permanent," he said and walked to the bathroom.

Daisy started sobbing again in a noisy way. She was breathing in short breaths. The dog instantly smelled her emotional state. He picked up a tennis ball with his mouth and dropped it at her feet, showing his compassion.

Daisy smiled through her tears. "Sugar, I missed you so much!" She exclaimed as she kissed the dog on the head.

Entering her room, she threw herself on the bed. She stretched out her arm and grabbed her mother's picture from the bedside table. She tightly pressed the picture against her heart. "I know you wanted to see me happy. I'm sorry if I upset you. I made a mistake by rushing into a marriage, but lesson learned." she sighed. "I promise I won't get married until I know my partner well enough." Daisy kissed the photo and put it back on the bedside table. She closed her eyes and dozed off without much effort.

Her sleep was quickly disturbed by her father. Robert tapped her on the shoulder and turned her sharply to face him. "Daisy, wake up!"

She rubbed her eyes, wondering if she were awake or still asleep. "What is happening, Dad?"

"Come with me, I think the dog doesn't feel well," he said, breathing quickly.

Daisy hopped off the bed in a second. She followed her father into the dining room. Sugar was lying on the carpet. He was shaking, struggling to catch his breath. "Oh, my God! What's wrong with you, my little buddy!?" She petted him gently on the head. The dog's breathing became shallow and uneven. Sugar tried to get up and move around, but he tripped over his front feet. He let out a pitiful whine. He looked dehydrated, his gums were white and sticky. Daisy placed a water bowl in front of him, but the dog refused to drink. "Dad, we need to take him to the Vet hospital immediately," she said as she rubbed ice cube on the dog's mouth.

"Sure," replied Robert. He put his hand underneath the dog's chest, scooped the other hand under the rump and lifted him with care. He put the dog in the back seat of his car and strapped him in safely. Daisy sat next to the dog. "Stay with me, Sugar. You will be fine, just hang in there," she said in a soft and soothing tone.

Daisy rolled the car window down. Sugar stuck his head out. It seemed he enjoyed the wind blowing on his face or maybe he loved the sensation of the air moving through its fur.

As they approached the Vet hospital, Daisy gave her dog a long hug. The veterinary surgeon took the dog to the back room for exams. Daisy was so nervous she couldn't sit still; she began to pace to and fro in the waiting room. "Dad, why did they take Sugar to the back room?" She asked, her voice sounded weak and breathy.

"I have no idea what goes on behind those closed doors." He shrugged his shoulders.

Daisy saw a nurse passing through the corridor and quickly walked towards her. "I worry so much about my dog, could you please tell me why does a doctor check-up take so long?"

"I understand your concern," said the nurse. "The doctor put your dog on a drip."

"Can I see him?" Daisy asked and pressed her palms together." Please," she said with pleading eyes.

"Sure," replied the nurse and motioned Daisy to follow her.

Sugar was lying on the exam table with a catheter inserted into his vein. Daisy noticed that a small part of his front leg was shaved for the IV. Sugar looked calm; he was breathing normally. "You are a Champion!" Daisy exclaimed and kissed the dog, then quickly turned to the nurse and said: "I think my dog feels much better. Can we take him home?"

"You need to see the doctor. She will openly tell you about his condition," said the nurse and walked out of the exam room.

Daisy felt so scared, she began biting her nails. Her mind was racing with negative thoughts. She knew she had to think positive to attract positive energy, but she couldn't control herself.

A few minutes later, the doctor in a blue uniform entered the exam room and greeted her. Daisy gave her an expectant glance. "Is everything alright?' She asked.

The doctor coughed awkwardly: "I'm really sorry to have to say this, but your dog is very sick."

"But he seems to be fine," Daisy interrupted her.

The doctor sighed deeply. "He is bleeding internally, it's a kidney cancer. I'm afraid we won't be able to save him. Unfortunately, we have to put him down," she said and lowered her face.

Daisy felt buzzing in her ears. Her mouth was dry, her throat closed up. She had a feeling the room started spinning around her.

"Are you okay?" The doctor asked her.

Daisy didn't reply. She put her head down on the exam table and silently screamed. She was in so much pain that the sound couldn't escape her mouth. The dog sensed her sorrow and bathed her face with his tongue. Daisy kept cuddling and smelling him, trying to keep the scent of him in her memory forever. "He smells like home to me, it's such a comforting smell." She sighed.

"Your dog knows you love him and he is grateful that you gave him a happy life," replied the doctor. "I'm so sorry that you are facing this, but you need to sign the euthanasia constant form."

"I will inform my father," Daisy said in a low voice, trying to collect her thoughts. She took off her cardigan and covered the dog with it.

"Sugar, I will always love you. You made my life so beautiful. Even looking at you made me happy," she whispered in his ear and walked out of the exam room, hanging her head down.

Robert was sitting in the waiting room. He quickly stood up when he saw his daughter. "How is Sugar?" He asked in a cracked voice.

Daisy looked at him with blank expression. "Dad, you need to say final goodbye to him," she murmured.

Robert rushed into the exam room. Daisy wanted to cry so much, but tears didn't come out of her eyes. She went out for a fresh air as she struggled to breathe. She inhaled deeply, though she couldn't get enough oxygen into her lungs. She had a feeling the top layer of her skin has been removed. Everything felt so sensitive.

Fifteen minutes later, Robert came out of the Vet hospital. He had a swollen face and bright red nose. Daisy noticed blood vessels in his eyes. None of them said anything. They sat in the car and drove off. Daisy held the dog's leash tightly in her hand. She rolled down the car window and poked her head out.

The heavy silence was broken by Robert: "We need to pick up the dog's ashes next week," he said and let out a long, loud breath.

Daisy scratched her arms as hard as she could with her nails to stop herself from screaming.

When she got home, she lit a candle and momentarily felt very close to her dog. Opening the window, she looked up at the sky. She saw a bright pink light hitting the clouds. "Oh, Sugar! I know you have crossed the rainbow bridge," she said and licked the salty teardrop from her upper lip. She curled up in the exact same way she used to do when she was little. She tried to fall asleep, but her mind refused to stop thinking about the terrible thing that had happened.

Daisy didn't get up from bed in the morning. She was lying with the blanket over her head. Robert knew his daughter was so depressed, she wouldn't eat. He made her favourite breakfast and entered her room. He put a plate with a honeyed goat cheese sandwich on her bedside table and tapped her gently on the shoulder. Daisy didn't respond as if she had a zip sewn over her mouth. Robert pulled the blanket off her face. He guessed she was awake by the way she was breathing. "Don't be so stubborn. You should eat something," he said and walked out of the room.

Daisy opened her eyes. The room seemed so silent and sad. No sounds greeted her happily in the morning. There was no wagging tail at all. No one was excited to rise and spin alongside her, hoping to get a treat. It seemed to her she was living in a dead house. She closed her eyes in attempt to escape the reality into sleep.

Time passed in a very painfully slow manner. The gloomy days stretched into a week. Daisy didn't step foot outside her home. Her phone was switched off, so nobody could reach her. She was practically glued to bed.

When her father showed her the ceramic urn holding her beloved dog's ashes, she experienced mixed emotions. She felt sad and relieved at the same time. The reason that made her get out of bed was the strong desire to honour her furry friend's memory in a meaningful way.

"I got permission from the local council to scatter ashes in the ocean as you wished," said Robert to her.

Daisy nodded in agreement and approached the place where Sugar used to curl up in a ball. She touched the spot, it seemed to her it was warm as if the dog were lying right there a minute ago.

It was a sunny day, not even a light breeze stirred the air. Daisy and her father were ready to say final goodbye to their loved one. The boat rocked gently from side to side as they boarded. Daisy was holding the urn tightly against her chest. Robert put his comforting arm around his daughter's shoulder. "Sugar became a very important part of my family. I treated him like a child. He was depended on me, but in some ways, I depended on him just as much," Robert's voice was strained. "Sugar eased my loneliness and brought companionship to my life."

Grief overwhelmed Daisy completely. It felt like a bad dream she wanted to shake off. The boat carried them three nautical miles from the shore. Daisy unscrewed the urn: "My dear Sugar, it's time to return to nature," she said and slowly scattered ashes into the water. Her eyelids spread the sparkling tears around her eyes as she blinked.

***

The new day brought a surprise to Daisy. She was awoken by the jingling sound of the doorbell. Sliding her feet into a pair of rubber slippers, she marched towards the front door. Daisy peered sneakily into the spy hole and saw her friends, Grace and Leo standing on her doorstep. She quickly pulled her hair back into a tight ponytail and opened the door.

"Did you really think you could escape and hide from us?!" Leo exclaimed as he put his hands on his hips.

Daisy gave him a little smile. "I missed you guys so much," she said and gestured for them to come in.

Under her smile Leo read the sadness in her eyes. Daisy guided her friends into the dining room. Leo threw himself down on the sofa. "D, would you make a cup of coffee for me?" He asked.

"Sure, I will treat you to strong black coffee and a piece of apple pie," she replied and walked out of the room.

Grace pulled a box of chocolates out of her bag and placed it on the coffee table. "I think Daisy has lost weight," she said to Leo in a very low voice.

"She looks like skin and bones. I guess going through a breakup must be traumatic," replied Leo and glanced at the door.

Daisy entered the room carrying a wooden serving tray. "If I knew you were coming, I would have prepared something delicious for you," she said as she placed the tray on the table.

Leo rolled his eyes at her, "But you cut all communication with us without explanation."

"I'm so sorry, I went through the worst period of my life," said Daisy in a quivering voice.

"It's a pity you broke up with Eddie, but why do you keep avoiding us?" Grace asked, impatience showing in her voice.

Daisy sighed. "Oh, I almost forgot I was married. I was devastated because of the loss in the family. I couldn't get over the death of my beloved dog." Her eyes filled with tears as she spoke.

Grace and Leo looked at each other with dismayed faces. "Oh, my God! I can't find the words to make you feel better," said Grace and gave her a tight hug.

Leo approached Daisy and squeezed her shoulder gently. "Sugar was lucky to have you as an owner and a best friend." He said.

Daisy let her tears fall. "Thank you so much guys," she said, still sobbing. Her friends let her cry and wash away all the sorrow and pain that had settled upon her heart.

Grace handed her a box of dark chocolates. "Try it, dear. Eating chocolate can help boost your mood," she smiled.

Daisy unwrapped the gold foil and took a small bite of chocolate. "You made my day special," she said as she wiped her tears.

Leo chuckled. "By the way, we have good news for you," he winked at her.

Grace opened her bag and pulled out a folded brochure. "Congratulations dear Daisy, you have been successfully enrolled in a creative writing short course," she said and handed her the brochure.

Daisy tilted her head quizzically. After a moment's hesitation, she said: "I have no idea what are you talking about."

'Let me explain," said Leo. "Ms. Brown thinks you have a potential to become a good writer. She wants you to take a course and pursue your dream."

"Well, I'm more than grateful, but I'm afraid I won't be able to afford to study." She sighed and placed the brochure on the table.

"You don't have to worry about it. All the expenses have been paid by our magazine publishing company," he replied. "I know you always wanted to be a writer. This course will be great whether for your career or just for pleasure."

Daisy pinched herself sharply on the arm and realised that was in fact reality.

Chapter Seven

The rain was falling in chaotic drops. The gusty wind blew the raindrops into Daisy's face. Her plastic raincoat didn't have enough protection for heavy rain. The water still penetrated through the large openings for her hands and head, even the inside of her old rubber boots got wet from stepping in a puddle. She had a feeling the sky opened up and ocean fell down.

Daisy reached the writers' school just in time. She ran up the stairs in a hurry. The tutor's office was down the corridor on the right. She poked her head in the room. "May I come in?" She asked the young man sitting at his desk.

"Please, come in. You must be Daisy Barton." He replied and gave her an intent gaze paired with a lingering smile.

Daisy entered the room with slow steps. The trapped water was making her shoes squeak. The noisy shoes made her feel so embarrassed. She scratched the back of her head awkwardly, avoiding eye contact with him.

The tutor stood up from his chair. He was tall with broad shoulders. His glossy blonde hair was slicked -back. "Jesus! You are totally drenched," he exclaimed and helped her take off her raincoat. "You will catch a cold if you don't remove your shoes."

Daisy sat down on a chair and popped off her boots and wet socks. Her feet had little holes in the skin, it looked something like swiss cheese. She blushed, turning scarlet as she met his gaze. The tutor chuckled softly, "I bet you have a swimming pool in your shoes," he said and shook water out of her yellow rubber boots. He stuffed a few bits of wrinkled papers in the boots to dry them out quickly. "By the way, I'm Lucas. I will help you with the emotional journey of writing your book," he stretched out his hand for a handshake.

Daisy gave a subtle smile. "Sorry, I have cold hands," she said as she shook his hand.

"Don't you know an old saying that cold hands equal a warm heart?!" He exclaimed.

Daisy stared directly into his huge deep blue eyes. An eye contact gave her an impression of his trustworthiness. Her hands instantly felt warm. Lucas smiled broadly, showing his bright white teeth. "Have you ever written anything?"

"Well, when I was little, I wrote a tale about the girl and the duck named Quaker," she replied, laughing at the sweet memory. "The girl befriended the duck by bribing it with bread crumbs."

"Sounds interesting." He arched his eyebrows in an inquisitive manner.

"Unfortunately, the cruel hunter destroyed the girl's happiness. He killed the duck with a shotgun. The girl found the orphaned duckling completely alone, crying for help. She decided to adopt the yellow duckling. She gave it food, water and stuffed toy to cuddle. The duckling still couldn't stop crying."

"How did the girl bond with the baby duck?" He asked with curious eyes, displaying genuine interest.

"The girl hung a mirror for the little duckling, so it looked as if another duckling were in the brooder," Daisy laughed." The trick worked. It made the baby duck feel safe. Little by little, the duckling got used to the girl and started playing with her. The funny duckling thought the girl was its real mother and followed her everywhere quacking in a high-pitched tone."

Lucas glanced at her with a soft smile on his lips. "I wish I had read your tale when I was a kid."

Daisy blushed. "You made me return to my childhood. Thank you for letting me experience this feeling."

Lucas gave her a prolonged eye contact. "I just noticed that you have a lot of cute freckles across your cheeks and nose. They are fabulous, they just give you an extra pinch of character," he said and grinned at her.

"Oh, I always hated my freckles and wanted so badly to get rid of them."

"You need to learn to appreciate and embrace what nature gave you," he said and flipped the page of his notebook. "By the way, when did you decide to become a writer?" He asked.

Daisy smiled and after a pause said: "When I was ten years old, I got very sick. My only companions were books. I found great comfort in reading. It took me nearly eight weeks to recover from a bad case of pneumonia. I was so grateful for the books that took my mind away from the real world. I thought to myself: 'One day I will write a book and will help other kids escape their troubles.'

"That was a very heart touching story and you tell it so well, Daisy. I think it's time to turn your dream into reality and start working on your debut book."

"I'm so ready," she said energetically.

"Perfect!" He exclaimed. "Focus on your book and deal with writing distractions. Please, don't try to find right words, just listen to your heart and be authentic. Develop various drafts. Sometimes when you are confused it means you are doing it right."

Daisy looked at him with her mouth slightly open.

"Don't worry, I will assist with the book writing process," said Lucas, smiling.

Daisy stared at him without response. She was lost in the depths of his blue eyes.

"You need to sit down and do the work. Books don't just write themselves. Take a few baby steps at a time. Write a sentence, then a paragraph and then if you are fortunate an entire chapter."

"I promise I will put my heart and soul into creating an important piece of work," she said in a way that left no margin for doubt.

"That's the spirit! I assume your dream is to become a best-selling author," he chuckled softly.

"Actually, I would love my novel to be transferred into a feature film. My dream is to see my invented characters on the big screen," she said. Lifting her sleeve, she looked down at her wristwatch. "Oh, it's a quoter past three. I'm afraid I went a little overtime."

"It was such a pleasure to listen to you." Replied Lucas.

Daisy pulled the papers out of her boots. "Oh, moisture is drawn out of them. My boots are dry and ready to wear," she said as she quickly put them on.

Lucas winked and smiled. "See you next Thursday at one o'clock."

Daisy nodded her head in response and walked out of the room.

The rain has eased off a bit. It felt like a sprinkle and left only a few water spots on her raincoat. She enjoyed listening to the rhythm of the raindrops falling on the ground. She pulled off her raincoat and let the rain shower over her.

As soon as she stepped into her apartment building, she opened her mailbox and looked inside. She found an envelope with her name on it. Daisy ripped the envelope open. Her heart skipped when she found out that Eddie had applied for the divorce...

***

Daisy bumped into Eddie on her way to the lawyer's office. Eddie looked different. He seemed he had gained much weight. His cheeks were so chubby he looked like a puffer fish. His eyes were cold, not showing emotion. Seeing him made her feel empty inside. She realised that she didn't feel anything anymore towards him. She felt discomfort behind her breastbone. The burning sensation moved up around her neck and throat. She felt sour taste in her mouth. She burped quietly behind her handkerchief, so he wouldn't notice. Releasing air from her stomach through her mouth gave her a sense of relief. She forced herself to greet him. Eddie whispered 'Hello' and lowered his head.

They entered the office building lobby and sat down in the armchairs opposite each other. Eddie buried his nose in his cell phone, trying to get rid of awkwardness. Daisy leaned back in the armchair. Momentarily she recalled her absurd honeymoon in extraordinary details. She got a queasy feeling in her stomach. She became anxious about not being able to stop throwing up. Daisy rushed to the bathroom and splashed cold water on her face. When she saw her reflexion in the mirror, she got startled. Her inner emotional state was written all over her face. She looked deathly pale and drawn. Her sagging upper eyelids made her look older. Her lips were colourless and chapped. She sighed deeply as she felt sympathy for herself.

When she returned to her spot, she saw him sitting in the same position, covering half of his face with his cell phone. A few minutes later, the tall woman approached them with a smile. She was so tall her head was almost touching the ceiling. She wore a wide belt over her black dress, emphasizing her tiny waist. "Good afternoon, guys. I'm Rosa Walker. I'll be working on your case." She said.

Eddie tucked his phone into his chest pocket and stood up from his seat. "Very nice to meet you, Ms. Walker," he said, trying to put energy into his voice.

Daisy grabbed her bag and rose up from her chair. Her mouth felt so dry that her lips were stuck together. Ms. Walker gestured them to follow her.

The lawyer's office room was extremely small, hardly had space for three chairs. It was floored with black and white checkerboard linoleum. The window didn't have any covering. The tree branches were brushing lightly against it. They were interlaced with one another, trying to enter the room without permission.

Daisy didn't want to sit next to Eddie, but she had no other choice. She had a feeling there was no air inside the room. She adjusted the fit of her skirt belt as she had shortness of breath. Eddie kept staring at his phone, a deep frown furrowed his bushy eyebrows.

Ms. Walker broke a heavy silence. "So, what is the reason you decided to get divorced?" She asked, resting her chin on her hand.

Daisy and Eddie kept silent. It seemed they were struggling to find right words to answer the question. Ms. Walker scanned their faces with curious eyes. "Well, I will help you to remind you of some reasons that might have destroyed your newly formed family: lack of commitment, infidelity, unrealistic expectations, too much arguing," she paused, waiting for their response.

Daisy scooted forward until she was on the edge of her seat. "We are worlds apart. We have nothing in common," she said, her voice pitched lower. She realised that her hands were shaking, so she buried them in her pockets.

Eddie raised his eyebrows as he glanced at her. Huh! We are worlds apart," he repeated ironically to himself.

Ms. Walker coughed softly. "Well, it's easy to end a marriage, but it's hard to save it. I would recommend you to take some time before making a final decision."

Eddie shifted in his chair nervously. "I already made up my mind. I want a divorce."

"So do I!" Exclaimed Daisy in a decisive way, not allowing contradiction.

Ms. Walker pulled the papers out of the plastic folder. "So, is that your final decision?" She asked and put on her eyeglasses.

"Yes!" They exclaimed together.

Eddie signed the paper that Ms. Walker handed him. He had a self-satisfied smile on his face. The corners of his mouth were upturned, showing how pleased he was about his own situation. Daisy took a pen out of her bag and with her shaking hand she signed the paper. She instantly felt peaceful and calm. Her mind seemed to have gained a freedom.

When they walked out of the office building, they didn't even look at each other. Eddie went left, Daisy went right. She crossed the street and took a relaxing stroll in a park. Daisy was full of optimistic expectations about her future. Her intuition was predicting happiness without conscious clues. She lay down on the green grass and stretched her arms to her sides. Looking up at the sky, she noticed the fluffy white clouds moving rapidly. In the blink of an eye, the cloud formed a shape of a dog. Daisy laughed loudly to herself. "That's my boy, Sugar! She exclaimed. She knew he was letting her know that he was fine. She felt blessed as she witnessed a special moment. She quickly caught the dog

-shaped cloud on her phone camera and rushed home to show her father the photo of Sugar floating across the sky.

When Robert saw it, he shrugged his shoulders. "This photo has a lot to say. It means the dog's spirit tried to communicate with you."

"Well, I think Sugar knew I needed to feel his presence as I had a really hard day. I signed the divorce papers today."

"You made a right decision. Do you know what happens if you don't remove a rotten tooth? He raised an eyebrow at her. "The infection may cause serious life-threatening complications. What I'm trying to say is that you can never be happy in a toxic relationship."

"I know, Dad," she sighed.

"By the way, you must be hungry. I will order two pizzas," said Robert and grabbed his cell phone.

Daisy nodded her head with a faint smile and went to the bathroom. It took her less than ten minutes to freshen up.

Entering the kitchen, she saw two open cardboard boxes with delicious pizzas. The aroma of tomato and cheese made her nose drill. "Oh, how did pizza delivery arrive so fast?!" She exclaimed.

Robert chuckled. "Pick up a slice and eat while it is hot." He said.

Daisy grabbed a slice of pizza and folded it in half. She held it with two hands for the first bite. "It is so tasty," she said with her mouth full. "Why aren't you eating, Dad?"

"I just got lost in my thoughts. I recalled the moment when I was sick and you fed me a slice of pizza with a toy fork. You were such a funny little girl," he said as he folded one end of the crust to another and took a bite.

Daisy gave him a thoughtful gaze. She realised that she discovered a good seed in his heart. For the first time in years, she felt that her father had a soft corner for her even when he was cold and distant.

Chapter Eight

In the early morning Daisy started writing her novel in bed to access the unconscious mind. She captured herself somewhere in between dreaming and wakefulness. Part of her was still in dream and another part was trying to adjust to reality. Daisy chose to write with a pen to get her creative mojo flowing. She thought her muse would speak better if she held a pen in her hand.

Writing process of the book came with emotional ups and downs. After completing the first few paragraphs she thought her writing was the worst. She felt she couldn't write a single word. She was disappointed in herself and threw the crumpled papers in a trash bin. She was going to give up, but soon a seed of idea struck her mind and a smile touched her lips. She started writing down what her inner voice dictated to her. Daisy became so happy, she began humming to herself. She thought she was ready to finish the whole book in one day. She really enjoyed escaping into fiction. Daisy felt inner peace as she got near the end of the first chapter of her novel.

Entering the writing tutor's office, she met his gaze confidently. She had a broad smile on her face. Seeing her smile triggered an automatic muscular response and produced a smile on Luca's face. "Your eyes tell me that you enjoyed the process of writing," he said, eagerly waiting to know what caused her happy mood.

"Indeed, there were moments when I experienced what the main character was feeling. I loved the fact that I was able to express myself and my ideas. Creative writing means freedom to me." Her smile got bigger.

Lucas squinted his eyes at her and grinned. It made him look more genuine and warmer. "Introduce your characters to me, please," he said and leaned back in his chair.

"Actually, my dream was to write a novel about motherhood. I had never felt the warmth of my mother as she died after I was born. I wanted so badly to experience the maternal bond with a baby, but my marriage was over in a blink of an eye and I couldn't realise my dream. I really wasn't able to write about an emotion authentically without experiencing it. So, I decided to write a book about a young hero who gave his life to save his friend in war."

"If I may ask, why did you get divorced so quickly?" His face turned red as he asked her a personal question.

"We just didn't understand each other." She sighed.

Momentarily their eyes met. Daisy got shy and looked away quickly. She pulled the green notebook out of her bag and handed it to him." I'm sorry that my handwriting is so sloppy," she said apologetically.

Lucas looked down at the notebook full of chicken scratch. "In the computer age you still write with a pen?" He chuckled.

"Huh! I'm just an old-fashioned girl," she replied, blushing and dropping her eyes.

Lucas held the notebook very close to his eyes. "Oh, I can't figure out what it says, because the letters are unclear. Could you please read it to me?"

Daisy seemed too anxious to begin. Her heart rate increased; she took a shallow breath through her mouth. She read the first sentence of the first chapter in a very low voice. Lucas leaned forward on a chair. "Could you please read a little bit louder?"

Daisy paused, she coughed nervously before continuing. Her face was buried in the notebook, though she could still feel his piercing glance. She got distracted and stumbled over her words. She tugged her mini skirt down with her hand and pressed her knees together. Lucas leaned back on his chair, trying to make her feel more comfortable. Daisy added more energy to her voice. She described the beauty of Afghanistan in such details as if she had already lived there for a while.

She gave him a quick sidelong glance to see how he was taking her story. Lucas seemed lost in wildest charm of tall, snow-covered mountains and the rivers flowing through the mountain gorges. Daisy's story made him travel to Afghanistan. In his mind's eye he vividly saw the soldiers carrying guns walking through a river and on a rocky ground. His eyes followed them to the military camp. The soldiers sat on the ground to eat flatbread. The old tea samovar was placed on the small wooden stool. Lucas inhaled the aroma of spiced tea. He felt an exotic mix of green tea leaves, nuts and saffron. A little Afghan boy with curly hair instantly caught Luca's mind. He was chasing his own shadow, giggling carelessly. While playing, the boy found a small box wrapped with a glitter paper hidden in the bush.

He quickly opened the box with big curious eyes. He was very excited to see a green toy tank. He jumped up and down with joy, but a happy moment lasted just for seconds. The booby-trapped toy exploded in the little hands of an innocent boy and instantly took his life.

When Daisy finished reading the first chapter, she gazed at Lucas and noticed a tear in his eye. Lucas wiped a tear with his index finger. "Your story blew my mind. It seemed so real. The worst and the most heartbreaking thing that a human has invented is war. So much is lost, yet no one wins."

"I absolutely agree with you. We destroy and kill each other without even blinking an eye. We contaminate the earth," Daisy said with a thoughtful expression on her face.

"By the way, who is the main character of your novel?" He asked.

"My uncle, Harry Barton. He was a war hero. He gave his life to save a fellow comrade. His army buddy shared with me the most emotional moments from Afghan war."

"Honestly, I listened to your story from the reader's perspective. I totally forgot that I was your writing coach. I can't wait to listen to a new chapter." He smiled.

"Thank you for encouragement and motivation," she replied and stood up from her seat.

Lucas accompanied her outdoors. "Can I invite you for lunch?" He asked her.

"I would love that, but I'm afraid I'm not available today. I have a meeting with the editor-in chief, Ms. Brown."

"No worries. We can hang out next time after class," said Lucas with a smile.

Daisy nodded in response and followed the narrow road with quick steps.

For the first time in a while, she felt she could breathe freely. She was more energetic, even her appetite came back. Her stomach started growling, begging for food. She looked around and noticed a small bakery shop at the corner of the street. She quickened her pace.

The bakery shop window was full of eye-catching cupcakes. Daisy stared wide-eyed and unblinkingly at mini colourful cupcakes. She mixed the ingredients in her mind and tasted them. She instantly felt increased flow of saliva in her mouth.

"How much is a cupcake?" Daisy asked the shop assistant.

"Three dollars and fifty cents," she replied shortly.

Daisy pulled her worn leather wallet out of her bag. She just found a five-dollar bill. She realised that a tiny cake wouldn't be enough to fill her stomach, so she bought a freshly baked loaf of bread. The golden-brown bread was still warm. Daisy broke a piece of bread and took a bite. She enjoyed a chewy texture and nutty flavour. Her teeth slowly crushed the rock-hard bread crusts. The roof of her mouth felt sore, her jaw went stiff, but she couldn't stop eating.

When she reached the office building, she ate the end piece from the loaf of bread. She quickly ran up the stairs and bumped into Ms. Brown's secretary.

"I'm happy to see you, Daisy," she said and kissed her on the cheek. "To what do we owe the pleasure of your visit?"

Daisy smiled. "I need to see Ms. Brown," she replied and pulled the piece of the bread crust out of her teeth with her tongue.

The secretary looked down at her wristwatch. "You need to hurry up then as she is going to have a meeting in twenty minutes."

Daisy rushed down the corridor. Ms. Brown's office door was open. Her long fake nails were clicking on her laptop keyboard as she typed. Daisy tapped gently on the door to attract her attention. Ms. Brown looked up at her and gave her a tight-lipped smile. "It's been a while since I have heard from you," she said and continued typing.

"I just wanted to personally thank you for your support. You inspired me to start writing my first book," she said and perched herself on the edge of the chair.

"You are welcome," she replied. "I wouldn't have suggested you to write a book if I felt you couldn't do it."

The pause arrived and made Daisy uncomfortable. Ms. Brown kept typing. "What are you writing about?" She asked without raising her head.

"It's about heroism, comradeship and love. I took your advice," she said. Her eyes were filled with tears of gratitude.

"Good on you. I think your inner self changed its colour. You don't look like a scared grey mouse anymore. You are ready to face the challenges for your dream. You associate with yellow colour which is symbol of hope and creativity," replied Ms. Brown as she gazed up at the wall clock.

Daisy knew it was a time to cut short the conversation. "You helped me to change my life for the better," she stood up from the chair. "I won't bother you any longer, Ms. Brown. Have a nice day," she said and walked towards the door.

"Wait!" exclaimed Ms. Brown. "Don't forget to bring me an autographed book."

Daisy blushed like a child. The sparkle in her eyes expressed her happy mood. "You will be the first person to read my novel," she said and walked out the door.

Through a glass window she saw her co-workers, Grace and Leo eating their lunches at their desks. Daisy smiled cheekily to herself as a funny idea came to her mind. She knocked on the door and ran off on her tiptoes before her unsuspected victims could see her. She hid behind the huge plant pot and secretly peered through the leaves of the tropical plant.

Leo poked his head out of the room. "There is nobody at the door," he said loudly and clicked the door shut.

Daisy gave a big belly laugh without using her vocal cords. She knocked on the door again and returned to her hiding place. This time Grace opened the door. She looked around the hall and shrugged, expressing her annoyance. "Who is playing a Nock and Nash game?! She exclaimed. After a brief pause, Grace walked into the room and closed the door behind her.

Daisy laughed silently, covering her mouth with one hand. The harmless fun provided a great entertainment for her. She rose from her hiding spot and marched towards the door. As soon as she knocked on the door, Leo opened it and took away all the fun. He grabbed her by the arm. "Gotcha!" He exclaimed in delight at the scene.

Daisy didn't try to justify her actions. She hugged him tightly.

"You are such a naughty girl!" Leo chuckled. "You didn't let us eat in peace."

"I'm so sorry," she said, still laughing.

The moment Daisy stepped into the room her grin faded. She saw a middle-aged man sitting at her desk. His white crisp shirt didn't have a single wrinkle. He was wearing the eyeglasses on the top of his nose. He was typing on his laptop, pressing the keys with hard force. Daisy glanced at Leo and quizzed him with her eyes. Leo felt awkward. He tucked his hands in his back pockets and said: "Daisy, let me introduce you to our new co-worker, Mr. Bloom. He is a very experienced journalist; he has just joined our team."

Mr. Bloom stopped typing and glanced up at Daisy. He gave her a nod of greeting. Daisy smiled in response. Leo and Grace looked at each other with puzzled expression on their faces. After an awkward interaction, Grace approached Daisy and whisked her off to the veranda to have a little chat. Leo grabbed two lunch containers and followed them. "Daisy, don't you want to try my salad?" He asked, smiling.

"No, thank you. I'm good." She replied.

"Maybe you would like to try some creamy garlic chicken with rice," Grace winked at her.

Daisy shook her head side to side.

"You better make up your mind before I finish my lunch. "Grace grabbed the lemon and squeezed it onto chicken until it was completely dry. She picked up a piece of chicken and held her hand out to admire it.

"It looks delicious, but I'm full. I ate a whole loaf of bread this morning." Said Daisy.

"What?!" Leo exclaimed. "I can't eat even one slice of bread a day. What made you so hungry?" He chuckled softly.

"I think excitement made me hungry," she said with a smile." I read the first chapter of my novel to my writing coach as I needed my professional feedback. I didn't want to read the lines mechanically, I needed to convey my emotions realistically. I tried to put my reader in the character's place in the story. To be honest, I put more energy and power into my reading than writing."

"I'm so proud of you." Said Leo.

"I think you were born to write. You deserve to realise your dream," said Grace and gave her a loving embrace.

"Thank you for the kind words, guys. Your lunch break is almost over, I will get out of your hair now." Said Daisy.

Leo took a step forward and grabbed her arm to stop her. "Before you go, I want to tell you something. Please, don't get sad that someone else is sitting at your desk. Your place isn't here, honey. You need to chase your dreams. Ms. Brown believes that you are very talented and special. Finish your book, unleash your talent and show it to the world."

"Thank you," said Daisy with a smile and tears in her eyes.

***

Daisy was moved by the desire to touch the heart of her readers. She wanted to heal people through her art. She wanted to show them that they were understood and whatever difficulties they had experienced in life, there was someone who was experiencing them too. The writing process helped her grow mentally. Every day mattered to her as it was infused with meaning.

When the second chapter has told its part of the story, she grinned from ear to ear. Daisy applied red lipstick to her broad smiling lips. She pulled her hair up in a bun and in a few minutes, she was ready for her writing class.

Walking out the front door, Daisy bumped into her father. Robert looked at her with penetrating gaze. "Why did you paint your lips red? Is there any special occasion today?"

Daisy blushed and looked down. "Nope, I just wanted to look good and boost my confidence. By the way, Dad, I will be late today. Please, don't worry about me," she said without looking at him and quickly ran down the stairs.

As soon as she reached her destination, she pulled the small mirror out of her bag and applied another layer of the lipstick.

Lucas welcomed her with a wide smile. His smile gave her chills. He gestured for her to take a seat. "So, how did your week go?

"Well, I never stopped writing."

"I'm ready to get to know new characters in your book," he said and made himself comfortable in a chair, crossing his one leg over the other.

Daisy opened her notebook and began reading the second chapter with emotions. She even made her voice deeper to impress him. Lucas started laughing silently. He tried to avoid notice, but failed in his attempt. His chair made a cracking sound as his whole body was shaking with laughter. Daisy stopped reading and gave him a stern glance. Lucas couldn't stop, he gave a deep bass guffaw. "I'm sorry, Daisy. I can't control myself," he said, still laughing. "Could you please get red lipstick off your teeth?"

Daisy quickly pulled a mirror out of her bag and looked at her teeth. She saw the crimson red lipstick stuck to her front teeth. She felt so embarrassed, she wanted to hide herself away. She closed her mouth and licked the lipstick off with her tongue. "I can imagine how funny I must have looked," she said, blushing.

"Oh, you just made me laugh so hard! You are the cutest person I have ever met."

Daisy gave a little smile, her lips remained closed.

"Please, continue reading," said Lucas in a tone that sounded calm.

Daisy took a deep breath and continued reading where she had left off. She revealed her main character's appearance through the interaction with the scene. Lucas vividly saw a young soldier in unbuttoned army jacket, painting the small house on wheels pink. The sweat dripped off his freckled face and raced down his sculpted chest. Lucas visualized the newly painted walls in his mind's eye.

The strong smell of paint made him dizzy. His eyes started itching and he kept on rubbing them. The burning sensation was completely gone when a new character appeared in the story. The crown braided woman instantly got in the centre of his attention. She wiped the sweat from the soldier's face with her handkerchief. The soldier gently kissed her bare arm. His glistening eyes spoke louder than words. Lucas was hearing his heartbeat in his ears. It seemed to him the soldier was having a love attack.

Daisy paused to catch her breath and then continued reading the story. Lucas was listening to the soldier's love poem with his mouth slightly open. He was reconciling the lines in the poem with the feelings in his heart.

When Daisy finished reading the second chapter, she looked at him expectantly, waiting for a compliment. Lucas scratched his head. "I see the resemblance between you and your uncle," he said with a serious expression. "You inherited literary talent and freckles from him," he said, chuckling softly.

Daisy laughed with him. Sharing the laughter signals made them realise that they looked at the world in the same way. Their sense of emotional connection instantly boosted. Lucas handed her a water bottle, "Your mouth must be dried out."

"Oh, you just read my mind. That's exactly what I needed most," she said and gulped down the cold water.

"Can I give you an advice?" He asked.

Daisy nodded in approval and stared at him with wide eyes.

"The only thing missing was the female character's personality. You need to dig deeper emotionally. The more you know your characters, the better you reveal them."

"You are absolutely right. I didn't know anything about my uncle's girlfriend, that's why her personality in the story wasn't displayed fully," she said with a regret in her voice.

"You should never leave important things out of your novel just because they seem hard for you to write. If I were you, I would look for her. She could share some inspiring moments and help you to write a compelling climax for your story."

"I think it would be hard to find her. I only know that she lived in the heart of Katoomba town. Her tiny house on wheels was painted pink by my uncle."

"I guess we have enough information for a good investigation."

Daisy smiled with her eyes.

"We will find her together," said Lucas with self-assured tone and rose from his seat. "By the way, do you remember the promise you made?"

"Sure, let's have some lunch together," she said without hesitation.

Lucas grabbed her by her hand and gently pulled her up to her feet.

They walked down the street arm in arm. His nearness made her feel comforted and relaxed. When Lucas interlocked fingers with hers, she felt a deeper emotional and physical connection to him. Her sensual switches were sparked. His touch made her go week in her knees. So nice this walk felt, so romantic. She hadn't felt so special in a very long time.

The small restaurant looked fabulous. It was lavishly decorated with terracotta clay statues. The dining room was divided into open area and cosy dining boots which were separated from each other with crystal bead curtains. As they walked in the doorway, Daisy inhaled the sweet and warm aroma of vanilla beans and slowly let it out. They stood there holding their hands, waiting to be seated. "Such a nice place. I have never heard of it," said Daisy as she scanned the entire room.

"It's a newly opened restaurant." Replied Lucas.

The hostess approached them with a welcoming smile. "Would you prefer to sit inside or outside?" She asked.

"Outside!" They exclaimed together and laughed out loud at their synchronized thought.

The hostess took them to the table overlooking the ocean. Daisy closed her eyes and listened to the waves continuously rolling in and out. Lucas has been thoughtful for some time. He was trying to hear her feelings. "I assume your brain loves ocean," he interrupted her thoughts.

"It makes me calmer and more creative," she said without opening her eyes. She popped off her shoes as they caused pressure on her toes and sighed in relief.

A few minutes later, the waiter came to their table with a water jar filled with lemons and fresh mint. He poured the water in the glasses and placed menus in front of Daisy and Lucas. It didn't take them long to choose food from a menu.

"I would like to try fish and chips," said Daisy as she closed her menu.

"The same for me," Lucas said quickly.

The waiter pulled out a red pad from his apron and jotted down an order. As he walked away, Lucas leaned forward on his chair and drew it closer to her. They enjoyed sitting silently in the shade of an umbrella above their heads. Lucas looked deeply into her big brown eyes. "I'm getting good vibes from you," he said without taking his eyes off her.

Daisy smiled and bit her lower lip. "I'm also enjoying your presence," she replied. She nervously reached for the glass and accidently spilled water on her legs. "Oops! She exclaimed. "I'm so clumsy."

"It's okay," said Lucas and grabbed a napkin. He gently wiped water from her legs. His touch gave her goosebumps all over her body. Lucas noticed little bumps on her skin. "Are you cold?" He asked.

"I'm fine," she said and pulled down her skirt.

The waiter returned to their table carrying a large tray. Lucas squealed with delight when he saw a tray full of food. "There is nothing better than fried fish, potato chips and of course the smell of sea. It never goes out of fashion," He picked up the napkin and put it on his lap.

"I agree. Fish and chips conjure up fond childhood memories of sitting in the park with my uncle. He used to feed me potato chips with his hands and that felt like he was giving me his love," Daisy blew on the chips to cool them.

"Your uncle would be very proud of you if he were alive."

"I will always keep his memory alive," she said with a slow nod of her head. "So good that you motivated me to find his girlfriend. Uncle Harry loved her so much. He had kept her picture in his chest pocket until he died. I'm afraid nowadays no one really falls in love," she sighed sentimentally.

"You will believe in true love when you meet your soulmate," he held her gaze for a few seconds.

"Did you ever experience true love?" She asked.

"Yes, I was madly in love. My girlfriend passed away two years ago," He paused, his melancholic eyes confirmed that the memories came flooding back to him.

"Oh, I'm so sorry for your loss," she put her hand on top of his.

"Anna died of leukemia. She was the purpose of my life. We lived through our triumphs and challenges. We faced life's uncertainties together. We knew each other's heart and soul. We celebrated life together," his voice cracked out as he was about to cry.

It was the saddest voice Daisy had ever heard. She handed him a glass of lemon water and said: "I think Anna was a happy woman as she was very much loved."

"On her deathbed she whispered in my ear: 'I want you to find a girl who will love you like I do', said Eddie as he wiped a tear rolling down his cheek with his finger.

The waiter came back to their table and interrupted their conversation. "Is there anything else I can get you?" He asked.

Lucas turned to Daisy. "What would you like for dessert?"

Daisy gently tapped her belly. "I'm too full to have dessert," she laughed with a chuckling sound.

Lucas smiled at her gesture. "As you wish. Let's have dessert another time," he said and glanced at the waiter. He made a writing a cheque gesture in order to ask for the bill.

Daisy gazed at the ocean with her eyes partly closed. The sunlight was reflected like a mirror by the water surface. "Thank you so much, Lucas for bringing me here," she said as she inhaled deeply the salty air.

"Actually, I wanted to thank you for letting me open up. I have never spoken to anyone about my pain," he replied. Lucas took a sip of water and paid the cheque with cash.

Daisy searched her foot around the chair until she found her shoes. She quickly stood up from her seat and raced down the stairs that led to the beach. She tossed her shoes on the sand and ran barefoot. The gold soft sand flew up behind her and stuck to her ankles. Lucas removed his white sneakers and ran after her. Daisy let her hair down: "Catch me if you can!" She shouted at the top of her lungs.

Lucas ran at full speed, though he couldn't catch her from behind. Daisy's feet barely touched the sand. She raced through the sand at a speed that rivalled a horse at full gallop. She streaked so fast that Lucas couldn't see her clearly from a distance.

"Stop! I give up," he exclaimed, wiping his sweaty forehead.

Daisy went into the water, giggling to herself. She pulled up her skirt as the water rose up to her knees. Lucas removed his shirt and rolled up his trousers. Daisy looked steadily at his broad chest and bulging biceps. She blushed as she found herself admiring his body. Lucas quickly went down in the water. "I'm impressed, Daisy. How the heck you run so fast?"

"Running is my superpower," she said in a teasing voice. Cupping her hands into the water, she playfully splashed at him and laughed.

"Aha! He exclaimed, waving his index finger back and forth. "I will teach you a lesson."

In the blink of an eye, he lifted her into his arms and threw her into the water. After a few seconds, Daisy pulled her head out of the water and took a deep breath. Lucas smiled, showing his teeth. "Are you okay?" He asked.

"Give me your hand," she spit salt water out of her mouth.

Lucas stretched out his hand to her. Daisy gave him a cheeky smile and dragged him forcibly into the deep water.

"The score has already settled," she said, laughing.

Lucas shook water off his head. He grabbed her by her waist and wrapped his strong arms around her. There was just a wet fabric of her dress between them. They paused and looked into each other's eyes deeply.

"I'm irresistibly attracted to you since I saw you for the first time. You looked so cute in a yellow raincoat and rubber boots, Ms. Barton," he wiped a droplet of saltwater from her chin with his hand.

Daisy pressed her trembling body against him. Her eyes wondered to his lips. Lucas embraced her tighter. He felt her warm breath on his face. His lips were inches away from hers, cascading onto her. Daisy felt her eyes flutter as she closed them. He caressed her cheek gently and planted a kiss on her lips. The kiss lasted for few seconds, but it sent shivers down her spine. The salty kiss seemed so sweet to her. Daisy's mind went blank. All she felt was warmth and comfort of his arms wrapped around her. It took her a moment to open her eyes. As she met his gaze, she immediately lowered her eyes shyly. Lucas smiled up at her sweetly. Lifting her into his arms, he carried her to the beach. They sat down on the sand. Daisy shivered in wet clothes sticking to her skin. She buried her feet in hot sand and squeezed the salt water out of her hair. Lucas grabbed his dry shirt and scooted closer to her. He gathered her hair in his hands and wiped it with it. Daisy felt awkward. "Oh, I have totally ruined your shirt."

"Don't worry about it. I have too many shirts."

Daisy smiled. Sinking her feet deeper into the sand, she realised that her feet were getting cold. Lucas noticed that her lips turned blue. "I really don't want you to catch a cold. We'd better get out of here," he said and helped her up.

Daisy shook the sand away from her clothes. "I enjoyed every moment I spent with you today," she said, staring into his blue eyes.

"To be honest, it's been a while since I've been so happy. I feel like a school boy again. I can't wipe a smile off my face when you are around me, " he replied and kissed her hand gently.

Daisy gave him a bear hug. "You are the only person with whom I can be myself. I showed you my soul when I read the first chapter of my novel to you. Revealing my hidden thoughts, I gave you my trust."

"Thank you, Daisy for putting your trust in me. Peering into your soul, I discovered your beautiful inner world."

Daisy flashed a smile at him. Lucas smiled back. " By the way, next time our class will be held outside," he said.

"Where?" She asked with genuine curiosity.

"We will visit Blue Mountains in search of the heroine of your book."

Daisy's eyes lit up like two shining gemstones.

They headed for the taxi rank. Lucas opened the back door of the car for her. He paid the taxi fare and asked the driver to take her home safely.

***

Daisy unlocked the front door to her apartment and rushed to the bathroom. The door was shut from the inside. She could hear the pitter-patter sound of the shower. She tossed the sand filled shoes in the hall-way and marched to her bedroom. As she passed her father's room, she noticed that he had left the light on. She stepped into room to switch the light off and was startled to see a blonde woman lying in her father's bed. Daisy put her hand to her mouth, expressing her shock. The blonde woman pulled the blanket closer to her neck. Her bangs framed her long face, playing a game of peek -a -boo with her eyes. Daisy glanced at the chair next to the bed. The blonde woman's dress was hung on the back of the chair. Her bra, panties and stockings were neatly folded and placed on it. Storming out of the room, Daisy bumped into her father. He wore only his black underwear which didn't fit him well. It was too small for him as his skin bulged around his hips. Robert was red all over his face and body with embarrassment. Daisy gave him a furious glare, her brows furrowed in one. She slipped her feet back into her shoes and went out, slamming the door behind her.

The sun was setting and it was getting cold. Daisy crossed the road and sat on a wooden bench in the pocket park in front of her apartment building. She felt so uncomfortable as sea salt crystals dried out her soft skin. She couldn't stop itching all over her body and head. She was scratching her scalp uncontrollably. Her fingernails were filled with sand.

A cool breeze made her tremble. Daisy pulled down her skirt which had dried salt stains on it. She rubbed her hands together for few seconds and blew on them to warm them up. The only thing she needed was a hot shower. She anxiously stared at her apartment building entry door, tapping her foot on the ground. She was waiting for the blonde woman to leave, so that she could return home. Daisy got thirsty and walked towards the small drinking fountain. She noticed a tiny brown bird filling its bill with water. The bird turned its head up sending the liquid to the back of the throat. The bird took just few sips of water using its dark grey tongue, then it tilted its head up again and sang sweetly. Daisy had a feeling a bird was grateful to God for the clean water to drink. When she came closer to the bird it flew away super quick as a wink. Cupping her hands together, Daisy filled them with water and took a sip. She licked her salty lips with her tongue. The pleasant goosebumps rose on her skin. She felt the urge to touch Lucas's lips again. She had a burning desire to be held in his arms. The muscles in her body started to get tense. Her heart rate and breathing got faster, her body temperature increased. She felt so warm as if she had taken a long hot bath.

Almost half an hour passed. Daisy saw her father's mistress coming out of her apartment building from a distance. The blonde woman got into the car and drove off. Daisy watched her until she disappeared around the corner. She opened the building entrance door and quickly ran up the stairs. Stepping into the apartment, she found herself facing her father. Robert was dressed in black sports pants and a white sleeveless t-shirt. His pants were baggy at the knees. He was breathing fast and hard. "Why are you mad at me?' He asked. He narrowed his lips so much that she thought he was biting them.

Daisy didn't say anything. She removed her shoes, avoiding his glance. Robert took a step forward towards her. "If you think I don't deserve to have a private life you are mistaken. I work from morning till night to put food on the table. I need to satisfy my emotional and physical needs."

"But why did you bring her home? You could have taken that woman to the motel," she said, letting out a sigh of irritation.

"That woman has a name. Lora is a decent lady. We met through a mutual friend. She is the one who understands me and for your information, I want her to move in with me."

Daisy turned pale. She felt sudden stabbing pain in her stomach near her belly button. "Dad, please don't bring her here again. I don't want her to take my mother's place," she said as she rubbed her tummy to relieve cramps and turned away from him.

Robert scowled at her. "Your mother is no more with us. We can never bring the dead to life. I need to move on and start a new life. It's my house! I will bring here whoever I want."

His cutting words pierced Daisy's heart hard like an arrow. Her eyes filled with tears. She felt a huge lump down her throat. She wanted to shout at him 'Shame on you!' But she didn't say a word. She pulled herself together and stared at him for few seconds. Robert heard a powerful roar in his daughter's eyes. She had the loudest eyes he had ever seen.

Chapter Nine

Daisy was up before dawn. She quickly brushed her teeth and rinsed her mouth with mint mouthwash, then she put on her favourite pink pleated dress on and looked at herself in the mirror. Spinning around, she glanced at her back side and adjusted her underwear with her finger to hide the embarrassing visible lines. Daisy walked into the kitchen with quick steps. Pouring coffee in two metal travel mugs, she glanced out of the window. She saw Lucas poking his head out of the black jeep wrangler window. He honked his horn and waved his hand at her. Daisy waved back at him. She put the coffee travel mugs into her bag and rushed out the door.

The morning sky was clear. The just risen sun cast the rosy hue across the sky. The golden fingers of sunlight touched Daisy's face. Lucas hopped off the car to greet her. "What a lovely morning!" He exclaimed and opened the car door for her.

"I'm glad we are having such a pleasant weather on our trip. It's neither hot nor cold," she said, smiling.

When Daisy climbed into the car seat, she felt that he was staring at her butt. She blushed bright pink and turned her face away.

Lucas settled himself in the driver's seat. "Are you ready for an adventures journey, Ms. Barton?" His voice boomed. It sounded like a party entertainer's loud voice, trying to keep his audience engaged and amused.

Daisy nodded her head twice. "I would never have managed this trip on my own," she said with emphasis. She pulled the travel coffee mug out of her bag and handed it to him.

Luca's eyes brightened. "You are the best, Daisy. I didn't have time to make coffee for myself at home," he said and took a large sip.

Daisy grinned. Holding the mug tightly in cupped hands, she raised it to her lips and sipped her coffee. It tasted a bitter-sweet way and it quickly heated up her body. Lucas jammed his foot on the accelerator and sped off.

The gentle breeze rushed through the open window and ruffled her hair. "Do you really think we can find uncle Harry's girlfriend?" She asked as she moved her hair to the sides of her head.

"My intuition is telling me that we will find her."

"Sugar to your mouth! Exclaimed Daisy. "I hope your words come true. Let's flip the coin and see. If it lands on heads we will find her," she said as she pulled a twenty-cent coin out of her wallet.

"I hope it lands with the yes side up." Said Lucas.

Daisy threw the coin in the air with snap motion. It spun around and fell on heads. She clapped her hands, laughing. Lucas laughed with her. "See, fate decided to be on our side," he said and pinched her nose.

After driving for about half an hour, he stopped the car at a rest area on the road. "Let's get some rest and stretch our legs." He suggested.

"Sure, fresh air will make us feel good," she quickly hopped off the car.

They walked slowly through the grove. In the middle of green trees and bushes they found a small cafe which was covered with lush plants.

"I'm starving, let's eat something." Said Lucas.

"This place is so inviting, I would love to have lunch here." She replied.

Daisy and Lucas sat down on a bench at the wooden table in front of the cafe. The waitress approached them holding a ceramic water pot in her hands. "You will be pleased you stopped here to eat. Our food will make you forget about takeaway," she said with a smile.

"What is today's lunch special?" Lucas asked her.

"Chicken burrito bowel with beans and rice." She replied.

Lucas glanced at Daisy with questioning eyes as if he were expecting to be given a green light. Daisy nodded her head yes. Lucas ordered two chicken burrito bowels and a jar of homemade dried fruit compote.

Daisy glanced at the bouquet of brightly coloured flowers on the table. She leaned forward to inhale its scent. Lucas drifted his gaze to the flowers. "You know, I have never given a flower to a woman as a gift. I think it's wrong to pick flowers because we are killing them. They have such a short vase life."

Daisy felt as though something stirred inside her. She felt deeper emotional connection with him. She gave him a little smile through her eyes and said: "I have been thinking exactly the same thing."

The waitress returned to their table with a large tray in her hands. She placed the bowels in front of them and a jar of fruit compote in the middle of the table. "Enjoy your meal," she said and went to the kitchen.

Daisy pulled a small bottle of hand sanitizer out of her bag. Pouring gel into her palms, she rubbed them together and handed the bottle to Lucas. He thanked her and squirted a small blob into his palm.

All of a sudden, the sky turned grey. Daisy glanced up, squinting her eyes. "Oh, the clouds covered the sky all over. I can't see any part of the blue sky anymore." She sighed.

"That's so weird. There was not just a single cloud in the morning." Replied Lucas.

A gust of wind blew the napkins off the table and whisked them towards the bushes.

"It feels like the sigh of the wind through the trees," said Daisy as she caught her plastic plate before the wind sent it flying.

"The rain is around the corner. We better quickly finish our meal," said Lucas as he took a bite of the piece of chicken breast.

The water droplet fell on Daisy's nose and startled her. After a minute or two, more droplets fell until the rain was streaming down. Lucas quickly paid the bill and put his jacket over her shoulders to protect her against the rain. They ran towards the jeep. Lucas helped her to get into the car safely, then he climbed inside. He buckled up and drove off.

"Let's not ruin our mood because of rain," he said as he turned on the radio.

Hearing her favourite song, Daisy turned up the volume and sang the lyrics loudly to her hearts content. Lucas laughed, "It's the song I sing in the shower," he said and began singing with her.

Daisy bobbed her head up and down, following the beat of her favourite song. Lucas tapped rhythmically on the steering wheel.

Meanwhile, the day became gloomier and the rain became heavier. The large raindrops were hitting hard the car windshield. The wipers were moving super fast, though they couldn't clean the screen properly.

"It's raining so hard I can't see the road." Said Lucas.

Daisy rubbed a little space in the steamed-up car window with her hand and looked through it. "Let's stop here and wait until the weather improves," she said and turned off the radio.

Lucas put the four-way flashers on and was about to pull over when he noticed a flashing hotel sign. He quickly parked in front of the two-storey hotel.

"Brace yourself!" He exclaimed and opened the car door. He lifted Daisy in his arms and carried her to the entrance of the hotel. Daisy was laughing heartily. Stretching her hands wide, she let the raindrops fall down upon her. The rain soaked her body, but she didn't care. She had a feeling it soothed her wounds and all her past misfortunes have been washed away.

The hotel receptionist greeted them with both palms pressed together. "You are lucky we've got a vacant room." He said with a heavy accent.

Daisy and Lucas glanced at each other without saying anything for a few seconds. Daisy felt uncomfortable staying in the hotel room with Lucas. She averted her gaze from him as she didn't want him to notice her nervousness. Lucas turned his head towards the host. "We will take the room for one night," he said as he removed his identification card from his wallet.

The receptionist checked them in and handed the room key to Lucas. "Sir, you are in room number nine on the second floor," he said, tilting his head side to side.

Lucas thanked him for his assistance. He wrapped his arm around Daisy's waist and whisked her off. He slid the room key into the slot and the door beeped. Daisy and Lucas stepped into the tiny room that had forest green walls and mint green curtains. Lucas whistled between his teeth. "There is not enough space to swing a cat in this room," he said, rolling his eyes at the ceiling.

His remark made her smile. She glanced at the single bed floating in the middle of the room. It was the narrowest bed she had ever seen. She felt a little bit uneasy and looked away, avoiding his gaze. Lucas threw himself in a black leather armchair. "The bed is all yours, Ms. Barton. I will try to make myself comfortable and recline slightly in an armchair," he said, smiling.

"Well, the bed is so small I'm afraid I won't be able to stretch my legs completely and the blanket is so narrow I have no idea how to wrap it around me," she said, laughing.

Lucas laughed out loud. "I guess all the funny memories from this trip will stay with us forever."

Drawing the curtains aside, Daisy looked through the window. The heavy rain was hitting the glass, trying hard to come in. "It seems rain isn't going to stop," she said with a little shrug of her shoulders.

Lucas pulled his cell phone out of his pants pocket and looked through it. "Don't worry, I just checked the weather forecast. It won't rain tomorrow." He said reassuringly.

Daisy felt relieved. Tension in her facial muscles went away. Lucas approached a little table with electric kettle and two white cups and saucers. He opened the water bottle and filled the kettle with it. "I will make us some coffee," he said, turning the kettle on.

"Let me take a shower first and then let's drink coffee together," she said and went to the bathroom.

Lucas set out the cups and saucers. He grabbed two sachets of coffee and sugar and dumped them into the cups, then he sat in the armchair, listening to the sound of boiling water inside the kettle. He closed his eyes and imagined Daisy's naked curvy body being hit by the hot water. His heart instantly started racing because of an adrenaline rush.

Daisy stripped as she stepped into the shower. Turning the knob, she slowly retreated to avoid getting the first surge of cold water that was already in the pipes. When desired water temperature was achieved, she started showering. The warm spray of water hit her skin, penetrating to the bones. Daisy had a feeling that Lucas touched her, moving his hands over every inch of her naked body. She let the water cascade onto her lips on a low pressure setting. She allowed herself to fantasize about Luca's lips mashing against hers and his tongue inserting into her mouth. She gave a little sigh of pleasure at the thought. As she reached for a bar of soap, she noticed a large dark brown cockroach on the floor. Daisy screamed so loudly that Lucas rushed into the bathroom without knocking and caught an eye of her naked body. Daisy quickly covered her private parts with her hands. "Lucas, please turn around," she said, still trembling.

Lucas turned his face to the wall. "What happened?" He asked. His eyes were tight and worried.

Daisy grabbed a white robe off a hanger and put it on. "I saw a huge shiny cockroach and got very scared," she said as she belted her robe.

Lucas gave a belly laugh and walked out of the bathroom. Daisy followed him with quick steps. "What's so funny?" she gave him a stern look.

"Oh, Daisy, I thought someone attacked you in the bathroom. I had no idea you were ambushed by a cockroach," he said, laughing. "Please keep your chin up, beautiful. I will destroy a cockroach nest." Lucas seemed confident in his ability to make a successful strike.

Daisy grabbed his arm. "Wait, I think if you kill the cockroach, its friends will attack us."

Lucas laughed so hard; his cheeks became sore. "I doubt cock-roaches have any kind of familial relationship."

Daisy looked at him with a puzzled frown. She couldn't understand what was so funny about that. Lucas pinched her cheek softly. "I made a coffee for you and almost forgot about it," he picked up a mug off the table and gave it to her.

Their hands touched and for an instant Daisy felt as though he touched her beating heart.

"Thank you, Lucas," she said as she perched on the edge of the bed.

He sat next to her. All they could hear was the pitter-patter of the rain against the window. Lucas stared into her eyes, then at her lips, then into her eyes again. Daisy rubbed her plump lips together. She blushed as her eyes darted to his succulent lips. He kept holding strong eye contact with her. His eyes were full of longing. Daisy opened her mouth to say something, but Lucas quickly covered it with his hand. "Shh! Please don't say anything, just feel it," his tender voice poured into her ear. When Lucas kissed her on the lips, her heart fluttered with happiness. She felt like her heart was a sponge, getting squeezed by his hand. Daisy parted her lips and kissed him back. She experienced the warm sensation through the whole body. Lucas kissed her softly on her neck, giving her new waves of pleasure. He inhaled her sweet scent. She smelled like fresh tangerine and he wanted to gently peel it with his hands. His eyes seemed to sparkle with pleasure every time he touched her wet lips with his. Pulling the belt loose from her robe, he kissed her chest. Daisy trembled as he squeezed her breasts. Her nipples hardened at his touch. He kept exploring her body. She moaned and sighed when she felt tingling sensation of his fingers teasing her belly. She was unable to resist him.

Lucas took off his clothes and pressed his body on top of hers. The bed shook, making a clicking sound. Lucas sprinkled kisses all over her body. The power of his strong arms made her feel desired and understood.

"You are so beautiful, I will never get tired of kissing you and looking at you," he whispered in her ear.

"Then don't stop kissing me." She murmured and sunk her nails into his back.

Daisy surrendered completely to him. Closing her eyes, she gripped the bed sheets and moaned in her throat. She drove him mad with burning desire. He loved everything about Daisy. Her freckled face, her soft skin, her scent and the cute sounds she made. He kept kissing her neck and shoulders. Daisy arched her body. When sexual excitement reached its peak, tears fell from her eyes. Lucas caught her tears with his fingers. "I fell in love with you with every bit of my heart," He gasped.

She grabbed his face with her hands and gave him a long kiss on the lips. She felt his pulse in the arteries of his throat. "I love you, too," she said, lowering her eyes.

Daisy fell asleep on his chest, still holding a smile on her face. Her brain was quite busy processing the positive emotions. Sleeping next to the person she loved made her feel calm and peaceful.

Morning sun's rays hit her eyes and woke her up. Daisy sat up, rubbing her eyes. Lucas was sitting in an armchair, drawing something on a sheet of paper. "Good morning, sleepyhead!" He exclaimed.

"I assume you were drawing me while I was asleep." she said and smiled at him.

Lucas smiled back at her. "I wish I could convey your exquisite beauty through art," he kissed her softly on the cheek.

"What are you drawing? Please, let me see," Daisy insisted. She scooted over to let him sit down on the bed beside her.

"I just made a sketch of uncle Harry's girlfriend's house. We can show it to local people and ask them for the directions," he said and handed her a sheet of paper.

Daisy sighed with appreciation. "Thank you, Lucas I wish I had met you sooner in my life."

His eyes flattered with contentment. "Ms. Barton, you turned my life upside down. I never thought I could fall in love with someone again."

They paused for a moment, gazing at each other's eyes. Daisy reached down and grabbed her robe. "I need to quickly freshen up," she said as she slipped into the robe.

"Please take your time. I will grab some sandwiches downstairs and come back," he winked at her and walked out the room.

Daisy stared at herself in the bathroom mirror. Her eyes were glistening with satisfaction. Her lips were so red as if she were wearing a red lipstick. Her skin was healthy and awake. It looked clear without blemishes. It seemed to her she has got younger. "Thank you, Universe for the gift of love. Now I believe in happy endings!" She exclaimed in delight. Humming to herself, she stepped into the shower.

After a minute, Lucas joined her. "I'm here to protect you from despicable cockroaches," he said. His voice pitched lower than it had been.

They both laughed, hugging each other. The hot water ran down their naked bodies. He bent his head and kissed her lips. "You are irresistible, Ms. Barton," he looked at her with an admiring smile.

Daisy blushed and looked away. She looked like a timid fawn, unsure how to respond. Lucas soaped up the sponge and started gently lathering her from her shoulders to her chest. Daisy closed her eyes, biting her lower lip with pleasure. He moved down her stomach and when he reached between her legs, she uttered a very low moan. The bathroom got fogged up. The steam from hot shower filled up her lungs. All of a sudden, Daisy felt suffocated. She realised she needed to get out of the bathroom quickly. "I can't breathe," she screamed as she rushed out of the shower.

"Please, don't panic, Daisy. I guess heat and moisture from steam gave you shortness of breath. Don't worry, you will be fine," Lucas tried to calm her down.

"I'm sorry for startling you," she replied, wrapping the large bath towel around her body.

"It's okay, my love," he said, smiling. Lucas quickly tied the white towel around his waist and followed her into the room.

The small table was set for breakfast. Daisy saw a tray of paper wrapped sandwiches and tiny bottles of fruit juice. "Thank you, Lucas for pampering me," she said and kissed him on the cheek.

"I just wanted to treat you to a romantic breakfast in bed, but they don't have anything fancy here," he said, shrugging his shoulders.

"You are the best. I couldn't ask for more." She opened the bottle of orange juice and gulped it down.

Daisy and Lucas ate their breakfast without hurry, enjoying each other's company. They were chatting happily and flirting with eyes. After having their breakfast, they headed to their destination.

The sun was shining brightly, there was no sign of yesterday's rain. When they reached the town, Lucas found a quiet residential area and parked his Jeep. Daisy stepped out of the car and stretched her arms up to the sun. "The air here is so pure and fresh. I wish I could catch it in a bottle and take it home," she said and inhaled through her nose until her lungs were full.

Lucas smiled, exposing front raw of his teeth. Closing his eyes, he breathed in deeply warm air. He held his breath for a few seconds and then slowly released, feeling the breath of life.

They followed a narrow path towards the bushland. Daisy was fascinated by the stunning blue haze in front of the tall mountains. "I wish I had a professional camera with me, so I could take beautiful landscape photos. The sandstone cliffs, waterfalls and canyons evoke sense of wonder."

"We can capture utter natural beauty on my phone's camera," said Lucas and took a picture of her against the nature background. Glancing down at the screen, he exclaimed: "Your smile reveals the beauty of your soul!"

"I think happiness makes people beautiful," she replied and gave him a wide smile.

They soaked in the serenity of the atmosphere. Daisy sat under the shade of a tree. She saw two medium sized birds quarrelling with each other. When a crimson rosella stretched up tall, a pale-yellow rosella sharply flicked its tail and spread its wings to make itself appear larger. Angry birds were making unique sounds. Daisy guessed they were fighting for a nest in a tree.

"It feels so good to absorb nature once in a while," she said and let her hair down to soothe the sore scalp from tight ponytail.

"Don't get carried away and abandon our mission, Ms. Barton. We need to find uncle Harry's girlfriend, remember?" he said and helped her up.

Lucas noticed an old man sitting on a bench, reading a newspaper. He pulled the sheet of paper out of his pocket and marched towards him with quick steps. "Good day, sir. Could you please tell me the best way to get to the pink house on wheels?" he asked as he showed him his sketch.

The old man shrugged. "I'm sorry, I'm not from around here. I'm just a tourist," he said using a slightly guttural 'R' sound.

Lucas picked up a French accent. 'Merci beaucoup', "Thank you very much," he replied in French.

The old man's face brightened. He seemed impressed that Lucas spoke in his native language. "I suggest you go to the souvenir shop. It's about two hundred metres away. The shop owner might help you."

Lucas gave him a thumbs up and nodded his thanks to him.

The gentle breeze stirred the leaves of the trees. Daisy quickly caught her pleated dress and stopped it from blowing up in the wind. She felt cool and warm at the same time.

Daisy and Lucas continued their search slowly until they reached a small gift shop. The shop owner seemed welcoming, smiling throughout. He was wearing a black Kangol hat and round sunglasses to match. Lucas handed him his sketch and asked for the directions. The shop owner removed his hat and scratched his half bold head, giving a sign of thought. He examined the sketch closely. "Keep going straight ahead and you will see it on the right," he said as he put his hat back on.

"Thank you, mate. We appreciate your help." Replied Lucas.

Daisy rushed out of the shop and ran straight ahead. Her heart began beating faster with every step she took towards the house on wheels. Lucas ran after her. It didn't take them long to find the tiny pink house. The bright pink paint looked faded and dull. Daisy noticed how old paint was cracking and peeling off the walls. The small windows were curved at the top. The windows were dressed in valance curtains, giving the house the tidy look. An aluminium door was left slightly ajar.

Daisy climbed up the few folding stairs and poked her head inside. She saw a woman with a dark burgundy scarf wrapped around her head, sitting at a small table. She was peeling the potatoes using a sharp knife.

The unexpected visitor startled her. She dropped the knife she was holding and gave a sound of fear. Daisy took a step back as she felt uncomfortable. Lucas quickly caught her arm before she stumbled backwards. He paused for a second and then gently knocked on the door with his fist. "Excuse me, ma'am, we would like to ask you something, if you don't mind."

"Come inside," she said and continued peeling the potatoes.

Lucas and Daisy stepped into the cabin and looked around. There was a narrow bunk bed full of pillows next to the window. The old books with faded and worn covers were pilled to the ceiling. Daisy inhaled the warm woody smell.

"How can I help you?" Asked the hostess.

Daisy gave her a polite smile, maintaining a kind of discreet distance. "Sorry for disturbing you, ma'am. I'm a journalist. I'm going to write about Afghanistan war hero, Harry Barton. I know that he was madly in love with a woman who lived in the pink house on wheels," she paused and glanced at her with wide, expectant eyes.

The hostess leaned forward in her chair restlessly and blinked her eyes. She shielded her face with one hand as if she were trying to protect her eyes from the very bright flashlight. After a moment's hesitation, she said: "Ah, the poor woman died of malaria." She quickened the rate of her potato peeling.

Daisy's smile faded. She tensed her shoulders and bit her lip with disappointment at the sad news. "Did you know her?"

"No," she shook her head and placed the peeled potatoes in the small bowel of water. Her fingertips were stained from peeling a bunch of potatoes. Daisy glanced at Lucas; her big brown eyes were full of sadness. Lucas took a step towards the hostess, trying to start a conversation with her. "Ma'am, could you please guide us on how can we get information about the woman who lived in this caravan twenty years ago?" He asked.

"I'm sorry, I can't help you with that," her tone sounded less certain. "I don't want to sound rude, but I don't have time to chat. I'm very busy." Her chin quivered as she spoke.

Lucas approached Daisy from behind. "I think she is hiding something," he whispered in her ear.

"I agree with you," she replied in a low murmur.

Daisy saw a stainless-steel water jag on the narrow dining table. "Can I have a glass of water, please?" She asked with pleading eyes.

The hostess adjusted her head scarf tightly and stood up to pour water into the glass. Daisy gazed at her, trying to read the emotions which flickered across her face. The hostess handed her a crystal glass half-filled with water.

"Thank you very much," said Daisy. "It's so hot outside, I got thirsty," she took a sip and licked her lips.

The hostess stared at her dress through her tightly squinted eyes. "What a lovely dress you are wearing," she kept peering with her eyes partly closed.

Daisy smiled, tugging up the corners of her mouth. "Thank you for the compliment, ma'am. I know my dress is a bit old fashioned, but I love it. It's very special to me. I have a feeling I'm experiencing absolutely different life through this vintage dress."

The hostess remained silent for a minute. She stared at her thoughtfully. "You look very pretty in this outfit. Can you turn around and show me the back of the dress?" She asked.

Daisy spun around a few times. She looked like a ballerina, pulling her arms in toward her body. Lucas laughed to himself as her pleated dress flipped up.

The hostess approached Daisy and gently stroked the fine material of her dress. She focused on the teardrop shaped pearl button up the back. Her mouth tugged in a faint smile. Daisy fixed the pleats in her dress. "It belonged to my mother. She died immediately after giving birth to me," Daisy sighed. "I wear this dress very often to feel her presence."

The hostess nodded in understanding. All of a sudden, she went deathly pale. She put her hand on her head. The muscles around her face tightened. "Sorry, I feel a bit dizzy. I think my blood pressure dropped down," she stumbled backwards and in a split second she fainted and fell on the floor.

Daisy screamed with fright. She tapped the woman on the shoulder, but she didn't respond. "Oh, my God! Is she dead?" Daisy exclaimed, glancing at Lucas with furrowed brows.

Lucas quickly squatted down and checked her pulse. He placed his index and middle fingers on her wrist, counting how many beats he felt in a minute. "She will regain consciousness soon, don't worry." He said.

Lucas carefully lifted the woman into his arms and carried her to the bunk bed. He used few pillows to elevate her legs above her heart. He sprinkled water over her face and loosened the scarf around her neck. The satin scarf slipped off her head and revealed the huge jagged scar on her right cheek. The pale pink scar went from the corner of her right eyebrow down her chin until it ceased to be visible below the collar of her blouse. The thick scar was raised above the skin. It made her look like she was mauled by a tiger.

Daisy stiffened and moved back. Her eyes bulged wide with shock. "I wonder what is the story behind her scar," she muttered under her breath.

Lucas was about to call an ambulance when the woman opened her eyes. She quickly raised her head from the pillow, covering her right cheek with her hand.

"Please, don't get out of bed immediately. You need to rest a little," said Lucas and handed her the scarf.

The woman wrapped the scarf around her head tightly. "I feel better now," she said as she sat up in her bunk.

"Ma'am, please tell us what you need. We can bring you some food and supplements." Said Lucas.

The hostess waved her hand hastily. "No! No! I don't need anything. Just stay with me a little bit longer, please."

Daisy and Lucas sat perched on white saddle stools. The hostess looked Daisy straight in the eye. "My ugly scar might have frightened you," she said in a calm voice. "I always try to hide it to avoid people's reactions and intrusive questions.

"I guess your scar is a badge of your strength." Replied Daisy.

"It was so hard for me to accept my scar. When the wound was still red and raw, I couldn't look at myself in the mirror. I remember once my neighbour's kids saw me without a scarf, they got so scared of me they ran away screaming. Gradually I learned to accept the destiny I have been given. Now my scar reminds me of how I overcame my pain," she gave a heavy sigh."

"I wish I were half as strong as you are." Said Daisy.

The hostess looked at her with teary eyes. Her fingers were shaking as if she were afraid of something.

"Would you like to share your story?" Daisy asked in a respectful manner.

The hostess was startled by her question. She lowered her head and gripped the corner of her blanket tightly, debating within herself whether to tell her a secret or not.

An uneasy silence was broken by Lucas. He reached down and grabbed an old book from the floor. The book cover was faded and smelled like smoke. "I see you are fond of reading, ma'am. You own too many books," he said as he flipped through the pages.

"When I have free time, I lose myself in books." She replied.

"What do you do for a living, if I may ask?"

"Knitting is my only source of income," she grabbed the ball of wool with a pair of knitting needles stuck in it from the bedside table.

"You must have a lot of work to do. We don't want to disturb your routine, ma'am," said Lucas and stood up from his seat, glancing at his girlfriend.

Daisy realised that it was time to leave and quickly got up from the stool chair. "We'd better take off now," she said and smiled fondly, crinkling her eyes.

The hostess paused for a few seconds, then she gestured for them to sit down. "I will tell you my story," she let out a sigh of pain.

Daisy and Lucas quickly sat back on their chairs. The hostess coughed nervously. It seemed that anxiety spasm caused a tickle in her throat.

"I remember the day in July of 2001 so vividly as if it were yesterday. I was going to attend Sunday Mass. On my way to the local church, I saw a plume of smoke and I knew it wasn't a good prediction. As it turned out the part of the five -storey hotel building which was under construction collapsed. The rescuers were going across the rubber pile looking for survivors. I noticed a construction worker wearing a yellow safety helmet sitting on a big stone. He looked so weak and tired, I thought he was going to faint. I quickly ran up to him and handed him a bottle of water. His shirt sleeve was soaked in blood. I used my handkerchief as a bandage. I wrapped it tightly around his arm to stop the blood flow from an injury," the hostess let out a deep, slow breath she was holding.

Daisy and Lucas stared at her, listening attentively to every word she said.

The hostess took a sip of water and continued her story: "It didn't take him long to find out where I lived. The very next day he came to my door with a thank you fruit-basket. I was pleasantly surprised by his kind gesture, impressed even, but when he started showing up at my place regularly, demanding to go on a date with him, I got annoyed and asked him to leave me alone," the choking heaviness forced her to pause for a moment.

"Why did you push him away?" Daisy interrupted her in mid-sentence.

"I didn't like him romantically," her eyes drifted away from Daisy as old memories flashed into her mind. "In a short while I found the love of my life. I met the handsome soldier on the dance floor on New Year's Eve and immediately fell in love with him. As soon as our eyes met, I knew it was him I was looking for with all my heart. It wasn't just his physical appearance that attracted me, I had a soul bond with him. I felt the energic ties that linked two of us on the cosmic plane," the hostess wiped a tear with the end of her scarf. "We confessed our feelings to each other and surrendered to love."

"Did you marry the man you were passionately in love with?" Daisy asked.

"No," she sighed. " He had to join the army. We promised to keep in touch with each other and write letters very often. I soon discovered that I was pregnant. I was so delighted to receive the greatest gift of life, but my happiness didn't last long," she lifted a glass with a shaking hand and took another sip of water.

"The construction worker didn't give up on me. One day he got himself drunk and gave me a visit. He could barely stand on his feet. His eyes seemed to lag behind as he proposed to me. When I told him that I loved someone else, he was so furious he punched a wall and smashed all the furniture, then he grabbed me by the arm and threw me on bed," the hostess closed her eyes softly.

Daisy noticed two tears that came out of her closed eyes.

The hostess continued telling her story, her eyes remained closed. "I cried and shouted for help at the top of my lungs. He ripped my clothes off and covered my mouth with his hand. That beast violently raped me for two hours, then he dragged me towards his car by my hair. He pulled me forcibly into his car and drove me to his place. He threatened to slit my throat if I disobeyed," she said with a sob in her voice and opened her eyes.

"Son of a bitch!" Lucas exclaimed loudly.

Daisy pulled a tissue out of her bag and handed it to her. "We didn't mean to bring back painful memories," she said with regret.

"Don't apologise, dear. You helped me to release emotions trapped in my body."

"Did the soldier know you were expecting a baby?" Daisy asked.

"He had no idea. It was such an irony of fate. Instead of telling him that he was going to become a father, I wrote a letter asking him to forget about me. After being sexually assaulted, I have been through hell. I was unable to stop crying. I even lost interest in life. I became a victim of forced marriage," she sniffed and wiped her nose with a napkin. "My husband thought he was the father of my baby. I couldn't reveal the truth to protect my daughter from violence."

Daisy leaned forward on her seat, craning her neck. "What happened to your child, ma'am?"

"One evening there was a knock on my door. I opened it and got hit by waves of emotions. My beloved soldier stood in front of me, looking at me in bewilderment. I was so shocked to see him, I stumbled to my feet and my newborn baby almost fell out of my arms. He froze for a second, his face twisted with sorrow. 'I'm sorry', I said, trying to fight back tears. He wiped a single tear from my eye with his finger.

He said he would carry me in his heart to the grave and stepped down the stairs slowly. As soon as I turned around, I saw my husband staring at me intensely. From the look on his face, I knew he heard everything."

Daisy and Lucas listened to her without interruption, absorbing every word. They were filled with compassion and pity for her.

"My husband punched a wall mirror in a fit of rage. It broke and cut him," the hostess continued. "In a blink of an eye, he ripped my baby from my arms with his bloody hands and put her on the floor. He grabbed me by the throat and pushed me against the wall. He hit me in the face so hard that my tooth moved from its position. I kneeled down at my husband's feet and begged him not to kill me with my child there next to me," she sighed in despair at the thought, wiping the back of her trembling hand over her eyes. "All I wanted was to take my daughter with me and disappear from his life. I grabbed the baby from the floor and began to crawl towards the front door when he slashed my cheek with a Stanley knife.

He left me scarred for life," the hostess softly touched the mark of misfortune on her right cheek. "He punished me unjustly. He took my child from me and stole my chance of motherhood. He didn't kill me, because he wanted me to suffer till the end of my life."

"Why didn't you go to the police?" Daisy asked.

"I knew my child was his hostage. I didn't say a word to anyone about his horrific attack to protect my daughter."

"Have you ever been in touch with your daughter since you left?" Daisy asked in an impatient tone.

"No, I didn't want to put her life in danger. I prayed to God to take care of her. I didn't commit suicide, because I knew I wouldn't go to heaven," she said, weeping bitterly.

Daisy took her hand in hers, showing sympathy. The hostess squeezed Daisy's hand tightly. "That's not all I wanted to tell you," she added. "When I met Harry Barton on the dance floor, I was wearing a pink pleated dress. I had sewed it myself. I'm more than happy to see you wearing it now," she said as she gave Daisy a piercing glance.

Daisy felt sudden, sharp pain in her heart. She quickly pushed her hand away and stormed out of the house. Eddie followed her out.

Daisy ran away from her troubles, from her fears, from her newly found biological mother...

She tripped on a stone and went sprawling on the path. Hot tears streamed down her face. Grabbing a tree brunch, she pulled herself up. She felt an earthquake in her heart. The explosion of energy within her. She stopped for a moment, trying to catch her breath. She leaned against the tree for support, burying her face in her hands. "No! She gasped. 'This can't be happening to me.' Anger surged through her. She clenched her fists tightly and pressed her teeth together in silent fury.

Lucas ran up to her breathing heavily. He didn't try to console her. He just wanted her to cry out and release her emotions. Daisy put her head on his shoulder and gave a deep sigh.

They walked along the path in silence until they reached the car parked down the road. Lucas opened the car door for her and helped her into the vehicle. "What can I do for you, my love?" He asked, genuinely willing to help her.

"Just be my calm in the eye of the storm," Daisy started crying bitterly. Large tears were flowing steadily down her cheeks. Lucas removed a tissue from the box and wiped her face with it. Her tears instantly soaked the tissue. Lucas removed another one from the box as she couldn't stop her tears from falling. He softly dried her eyes, but she blinked back fresh tears. He grabbed two more tissues to wipe her eyes and nose. He hugged her tightly until she sobbed herself free of tears and relaxed in his arms.

"It seems to me my whole life was based on a big lie. Everything I believed in was shattered," she said in a quivering voice.

"I know it was a great shock for you to find out your family secret, but please try to calm down," said Lucas in a firm-reassuring tone.

"Now my life seems like someone else's story. I can't accept that." She sighed.

"It takes time to deal with shocking news. Please be patient, allow yourself time to start a new chapter in life. Together we can get through this. We are a team, remember?" Lucas kissed her right hand, then her left.

"Oh," she gasped. "I feel so bad, Lucas. The man I have called a father turns out to be a real monster and my birth mother had been hiding all these years. I'm so angry at her. Why did she never try to reach out to me? Why was it so hard for her to gather her wits and courage and see how I was doing?" Her bottom lip quivered.

"I know your mind is racing with questions, but please don't torture yourself figuring it all out. Let the information sink. Try not to judge your mother. She did everything she could to protect you. When you are calm and ready to meet her face to face, have a sincere conversation with her."

"I can't think straight. I'm still in a state of shock. My life is a mess and I'm not able to handle it. How can I look at my father like I used to?"

"If I were you, I would have looked him straight in the eye and told him how I feel," said Lucas in an encouraging manner. "You have nothing to fear, my love."

"I'm so lucky that you came in my life," she leaned into him to kiss him and feel the warmth of his lips on hers.

Their lips pressed like magnets against one another. At that moment Daisy forgot about everything that had worried her and lost herself in his warm embrace. They kissed until they were gasping for air. For several minutes Daisy and Lucas sat silently, listening to their breathing.

"Are you ready to go home?" He asked as he buckled his seat belt.

She nodded her head and curled into a ball on her seat. Lucas started the car and turned on his radio to listen to soothing music. Daisy was so tired; she quickly fell into a deep sleep. He took off his leather jacket and covered her up with it, gently draping it across her shoulders.

It was a heart-rending drive home. When Lucas arrived at Daisy's place, he softly tapped her on the shoulder, trying to wake her up. Daisy gave a sudden jerk of her head and opened her eyes. Lucas caressed her cheek tenderly, moving his fingertips about one inch per second with a slight pressure. "Are you okay?" He asked.

Daisy rubbed her red eyes and after a long pause said: "Yeah, I feel a little bit better. I really appreciate you sticking with me through a tough time. I think I'm lucky one to have found a ride -or- die partner," She pulled the Jeep's door open and was about to get out of the car when he grabbed her arm. "Let me come with you," he said as he removed the car key from the ignition.

"No, I will face him alone. Please don't worry about me. I'll be fine."

"Okay, I will wait for you in the car. Pack all your stuff. I want you to move in with me."

Daisy paused before replying. "Are you sure about that?" She asked.

"I have never been so certain about anything." He smiled softly.

She gave him back a little smile before she left.

Entering her apartment building, Daisy raced up the stairs, taking three steps at a time. She stopped at her front door, letting her breath out. She had no idea how to start a conversation with Robert. Would it be better to yell at him and let go of her grudge, or interrogate him and get the answers to her most pressing questions. She was debating with herself when Robert opened the door.

"Finally!" He exclaimed wrathfully and gave her a stern glare. His forehead wrinkled as he raised his eyebrows at her. "Where have you been, huh? I was worried sick about you. I tried to call you, but your number wasn't reachable. I didn't know what happened to you, so I called the police for help," his tone turned aggressive as he spoke, demanding an explanation.

Daisy stared at him blankly. "Who are you to question me? It's time to take a mini holiday from your ego. You have no business asking me anything," she said sarcastically and stepped into the hallway.

"Like it or not, I'm your father. I was the one who did his best to keep a roof over your head, food in your tummy and clothes on your back. I was the one who attended parent teacher meetings at your school. I taught you how to tie your shoelaces, ride a bike, how to cook the prefect fried egg," he nodded his head emphasizing each word. The bubbles of saliva flew out of his mouth as he spoke. "You've got me worried only because I brought my girlfriend home. It's so grossly unfair to be disrespected by your own flesh and blood. Shame on you! You are rude and selfish; you are acting like a spoiled brat," he whined like a wounded animal.

"Shut up already!" Daisy raised her voice. "You mean absolutely nothing to me. You no longer have any power over me."

Robert eyed her in hostile silence. He looked like steam came out of his ears and nose. His face turned the brick red colour. The goosebumps made his hair stand on end. He took a step towards her and raised his hand to hit her, but Daisy caught his hand in mid-air. "Are you going to punch me in the face just like you did to my mother? Or maybe you want to slash my face with a knife and leave a huge scar on my cheek."

Robert stumbled forward into her arms. His lower jaw began chattering. The colour of his face changed from red to pale white. It seemed he felt out of his body. He squatted on the floor and leaned against the wall. "Ah! He gave a deep sigh and buried his face in his hands as he couldn't look her in the eye.

Daisy squatted in front of him. "Are you ready for an honest conversation?" She asked.

"Ask me what you want to know," he replied without raising his head.

"Did you know that my mother had an affair with your brother when you married her?" Her heart was beating fast as she asked him a question.

"No, she told me that she was in love with someone else, but I had no idea my brother was her lover. I only discovered that by chance when I overheard a conversation between my wife and Harry. He had promised her to love her till the end of his life. They were standing on the doorstep of my home. His passion-filled speech made my blood boil."

"How did you explain to him my mother's disappearance?"

"I told everyone, including Harry that she had died a week after giving birth from an infection. My brother often visited my house, so he could spend time with you. I assumed he loved you not because you were his niece, but because you were his lover's kid. Just before he went to serve in Afghanistan, he left a letter for you," Robert wiped a small tear from the corner of his eye with his thumb.

"Where is the letter?" Daisy's voice softened with concern.

"I keep it on the top shelf of the bookcase," he undid the top button of his shirt, taking a deep breath.

Daisy rushed into the study room. She hopped on a step stool. Standing on her tiptoes she reached the top shelf. Her hands were shaking when she grabbed an envelope with her name on it. She quickly opened the letter. It was written in an accurate handwriting, so it was easy to make out:

"Dear Daisy,

if you are reading this it means I couldn't make it home. I left for Afghanistan when you were six years old. It was very hard for me to leave you, because you were so special to me, dear. I live in heaven now. I want you to know that I'll be with you in spirit. I will watch over you and protect you every day. Never be afraid to face difficulties and fight for your happiness. I'm sure you will have a bright future ahead of you. Just have fun, enjoy your life and remember that I will always love you, kiddo.

Your uncle, Harry Barton."

Daisy pressed the back of her hand against her lips to stop herself from roaring in pain. She hugged the letter wetted with her tears close to her heart. She felt as if she were a baby, embracing him tightly. She closed her eyes until a foggy picture of Harry came into her mind. His letter was a balm that healed her fresh wounds. It gave her a comfort she needed. She put it back in the envelope and with slow steps went to her room. Daisy pulled the wardrobe door open and threw her clothes into the middle-sized suitcase. It didn't take her long to pack as she didn't own many clothes and shoes. When she took a quick glance around her room, she saw her mother's framed picture on the bedside table. After a moment's hesitation, she grabbed the picture and put it in her bag.

Walking into the hallway, Daisy saw Robert sitting on the floor in the same position. His eyes were red and puffy as if he had been crying for hours. In that moment she realised she wasn't experiencing rage, pain or sadness and it felt like a relief.

Robert coughed nervously before talking to her. "If you want to make a complaint against me, go to the police. I won't stop you. You can do everything your heart desires."

A long moment passed until Daisy made her tongue say: "I'm not going to send you to jail. I will tell you an ugly truth that will leave a deep scar in your heart."

Robert stood up, staring at her intensely, trying to read her face. Daisy inhaled deeply, gathering her stamina and courage. "My mother made a shocking confession to me. She revealed that my real father was Harry Barton. To be honest I'm happy to know that you aren't my biological dad," she said in a calm tone. She felt as though a heavy weight had been lifted off her mind. Daisy grabbed a suitcase and walked out the front door, leaving him in silent agony.

Lucas stood leaning against his car. When he saw her safe and sound, he relaxed and grinned at her. "Is everything alright?" He asked as he put her suitcase in the trunk of his Jeep.

Daisy nodded yes and hopped into the car. Lucas sped off and whisked her away.

Chapter Ten

Daisy woke up to the beeping sound of a smoke alarm. She wiped sleep dust from her eyes and yawned loudly. She sat up as she looked around the room. It was so scary for her to adjust to new environment. She felt anxious at the thought of a big change, even though she knew it was for the best. The bright sunlight streaming through the balcony door made her squint. When she got out of bed, the beeping sound got louder. She smelled something burning and ran to the kitchen.

Lucas was coughing, waving his hands to and fro to clear the smoke from his face.

"Oh, my God! The frying pan is on fire." Daisy exclaimed.

Lucas quickly turned off the stove and threw a damp tea towel over the pan to prevent a mess. "I'm so sorry, Daisy for chaos in the kitchen. I tried to make fluffy scrambled eggs with cheese and vegetables for you to put you in a good mood," puffing his cheeks out, Lucas exhaled a burst of air through his lips. "I guess I overheated the frying pan and it caused the flame," he said and tossed the burnt pan into the rubbish bin.

"It's obvious that your home lacks a woman's hand," said Daisy, wiping the bread crumbs from the edge of the table into her hand.

Lucas chuckled at her forthrightness.

It took her only five minutes to prepare breakfast. She toasted thickly sliced pieces of bread and spread butter and dark brown honey on them, then she made mug of black tea for herself and for Lucas. While squeezing half of a lemon into the tea, she accidently splashed the lemon juice in her eye. "Ouch!" Exclaimed Daisy, rubbing her right eye. "I feel a burning sensation in my eye and my vision got blurred."

"Don't worry, dear. It's just a temporary burning. I will rinse out your eye well. You should be fine," said Lucas and gently poured cold water over her eyeball from a glass. He continued flushing out her eye for a few minutes, then his lips brushed her closed eyelids very slowly. "Are you feeling better?" He asked.

"I could sit here all day enjoying your sweet kiss," she replied as she opened her eyes.

Lucas cupped her face in his hands and kissed her lips tenderly. Daisy felt love washing over her. She felt that she really mattered to him. She snuggled against his chest, listening to his heartbeat.

"Thank you, my love for preparing breakfast for me," said Lucas.

Daisy flashed him a big smile and passed him a plate. Lucas took a bite of the toast and looked at her. He was sure she was waiting for a response. "It is pure ambrosia. Without a doubt honey steals the show from the toasted bread and butter," he licked the drop of sweet honey from the corner of his mouth with his tongue.

Her cheeks flushed at his compliment. She made him another honey butter toast. Lucas glanced at her for a long moment with a gleam in his eye. "Did you know that Daisy symbolize purity and innocence? I think your character fits your name perfectly."

"And did you know the meaning of your name? Lucas means 'bringer of light' in Latin. Your name matches your personality. You uncover mysteries, bring light to the darkness and offer hope, compassion and kindness."

Lucas drank the last sip of his black tea. He sucked the air and the tea inside his body, making a slurping sound.

"I'm so glad we used a trip to Blue Mountains to do research for your book and get the answer mudded in uncertainty. Our investigation helped you find your real mother. Now your story will be authentic. I'm sure revealing the shocking plot twist will leave a memorable impression on your readers."

The smile faded from Daisy's face. "Actually, I have two requests: please, don't ask me to get to know my mother better and don't insist me to finish writing my book. I really don't think I can do that anymore.

I have no heart for writing. I have decided to make a career change. I will give up on my writing and start looking for a new job," she said in a quavering voice.

"Don't rush your decision, Daisy. Take a break from writing. You don't have to force anything. I will stand by your side and support you in every way possible," he said, leaning towards her. He gave her a butterfly kiss by fluttering his own eyelashes against hers.

"You kissed my with your eyelashes," Daisy chuckled. "It was the sweetest kiss I have ever had."

"I want to kiss you every second, every minute, every hour," he said, planting feathery kisses over her face. "My love, I'd better go to work now before you entice me into sexual activity," he laughed at his own joke.

Daisy threw her head back and laughed with him.

"You are so beautiful when you laugh. Please always wear a smile on your face," he pinched her nose gently. "I will be home by six. Enjoy your day. Have a little walk and get vitamin D from sun."

"I will sit on your beautiful veranda and get a nice tan," she replied, smiling.

"Of course, as you wish," he grabbed his car keys.

Daisy waved him goodbye as he walked out the front door. She realised her hands were sticky with honey dribbles. She washed them at a kitchen sink and stepped out to the veranda. It was festooned with passion flowers, orange marigolds and purple magenta blossoms. Daisy sank into the brown wood rocking chair and let the sun embrace her. She slowly rocked herself back and forward, enjoying the gentle motion. She was comfortable in her own little bubble. The golden sun's rays shone within her and warmed her skin. She closed her eyes and felt the light sent from the sky circling around her.

For the first time in her life, she experienced the feeling of being fully present in the moment rather than being consumed by her worrying thoughts. "Lucas is the proof that God really loves me," she murmured to herself. The thought of him made her heart smile. She spent about twenty minutes in the sun and it was enough for her to feel calmer and focused.

Daisy went back into the kitchen. She wanted to make her favourite pasta in a homemade tomato sauce for dinner. She opened the fridge to look for some fresh tomatoes, but she found none, so she decided to cook pasta with garlic and cheese.

Lucas arrived exactly at six o'clock. Daisy greeted him with a lively smile. Giving him a smooch, she cuddled him tightly. She put her hands on his neck and pressed her chest against his.

"Your hug is my home. It makes me feel warm and comforted," he said and pulled her closer to him.

"When you hold me in your arms, I just feel like you are a shield that protects me from danger," replied Daisy and wrapped him in a very tight hug that she didn't release.

"I will keep you safe until you allow me," he kissed her earlobe lightly.

Daisy gave him a wider smile. "Dinner is ready. Wash your hands and meet me in the kitchen."

"But I wanted to take you out for dinner. My bad, I should have informed you earlier," he said with concern in his voice.

"No worries, we can have dinner out some other time."

"How about we go to the restaurant tomorrow evening? I think it would be nice to ask your best friends if they would like to join us."

"Marvellous idea!" Exclaimed Daisy.

Lucas went to the bathroom with a self-satisfied smile. "Hey, do your friends like Italian cuisine?" He asked her from behind the closed door.

"Well, yeah. I guess so," she replied loudly so that he could hear her.

After dinner Daisy called Grace and Leo and invited them to an Italian restaurant. She couldn't stop herself from sharing her family secret with them. Touching her emotional wounds made her sad again. She felt as if she were rubbing salt in her wounds. Lucas noticed that tears formed in her eyes. He kissed her softly on the eyelids and shook off her sadness.

***

Upon entering the restaurant, Daisy and Lucas were greeted by the cheerful Italian folk music. Lucas put his hand around Daisy's shoulder and leaned in to murmur into her ear: "This fast-tempo, upbeat music makes me want to dance and sing out loud." His deep voice tickled her eardrum. Daisy giggled, rubbing her ear with her hand.

Grace and Leo were sitting at a corner table. Leo stretched his neck and extended his nose straight into the air, trying to get a better look at Daisy's boyfriend. He eyed him from head to toe with an open admiration that brought a smile to Luca's face. As soon as Daisy settled into her chair, she received a text message from Leo, saying: 'your boyfriend is so hot.' Daisy laughed to herself and stepped on Leo's foot under the table. Leo coughed, clearing his throat. "Lucas, I must admit that I have never seen Daisy so happy. I'm glad that you put a sparkle in her eye. It speaks of a feeling of love and be loved in return."

"Daisy came into my life like a breath of fresh air," Lucas took his girlfriend's hand and kissed her fingers gently. He gave Daisy a heated look so intense, she blushed.

A few minutes later, the waitress approached them and gave them a wide toothy smile. Daisy noticed that her eyes looked tired and lifeless. It seemed to her she smiled because it was part of her job to be friendly. The waitress handed each of them the dinner menu. Lucas waited for Daisy to order first. Daisy set her menu down without browsing it. "I would like to try a pizza Margherita," she said and returned the hard-backed menu to the waitress.

"The same for me!" Exclaimed Grace.

Lucas and Leo also seemed pleased with Daisy's choice. They ordered four pizzas and a bottle of Italian red wine.

"D, I stayed up all night thinking about your family drama. Lifting the veil of secrecy surrounding your mother will be a good climax for your novel, don't you think? Mark my words, your mom will help you to become a bestseller author," said Leo in an amused, confiding voice.

Grace elbowed him lightly to shush him. "Stop it Leo, family is a subject you shouldn't joke about."

Strained smile pinned to Daisy's face.

The waitress broke the awkward silence when she set down their pizza in front of them. Each pizza was sliced into four square pieces. 'Buon Appetite', enjoy your meal" she said in Italian.

"Grazie," Thank you, replied Lucas.

Leo looked at him with curiosity. "Do you speak Italian?"

"Well, I just speak a little Italian. I love learning a new language. I think it is like climbing a tall mountain. It seems difficult at first, because you need to memorise new words, but if you don't give up easily and keep fighting for your goal you will get the desired result. And trust me there is nothing more beautiful than a view from the top of the mountain."

"That was very well said, Lucas. You motivated me to learn a foreign language," replied Leo and turned his head to Grace. "What do you say, should we take Italian language course?" He asked her.

Grace shrugged her shoulders. It seemed Leo couldn't make her excited about his initiative. Her brain was focused on food in front of her. She gobbled down a slice of pizza and sniffed it. "Oh, I love the mix of tomatoes, white mozzarella and basil," she spoke with her mouth full. " I need to go on a diet, but I can't turn my nose up at this," she grabbed another slice.

Daisy laughed softly. "You don't need to lose weight. Just because you aren't a skinny toothpick doesn't mean that you are overweight. Embrace your body, Grace. By the way, men are crazy about curvy women," she winked at her.

"I know I'm sexy. I have more flash to grab onto and explore with hands," said Grace with a giggle. Her keen sense of humour made them all laugh.

After they finished eating their dinner, Lucas asked Daisy to dance with him. Daisy cheerfully followed him out to the dance floor.

At the thrumming rhythm of the music they began to dance. Pulling her close into his arms, Lucas kissed her on the neck. They stared at each other, opening up an energy connection with their eyes. Daisy enjoyed his strong arms wrapped around her and set her head on his shoulder. Lucas slightly tilted his head to the side and teased her with a little nibble kiss. As the music grew louder, he gently pushed her away. Holding on to her left hand with his right, he spun her around for several times. The upbeat rhythm increased her mood. Daisy felt as if she were flying and her feet were not touching the ground. She laughed loudly as her skin tingled and goosebumps formed. Her vision blurred by the flashing colours.

Leo and Grace were amused by the intimate conversation between Daisy and her boyfriend. Daisy waved her hand for them to join her. In a blink of an eye, Leo and Grace stepped onto the dance floor. Throwing his long arms out, Leo waved them rhythmically from side to side in tune with the beat. Grace was trying to mimic Leo's dance moves, but she couldn't make her dancing look less awkward. "I'm not a good dancer. I don't really have the cool moves," she said with a worried frown on her face.

"Take it easy, Grace. Just let the rhythm control your movements," Daisy encouraged her friend.

Lucas grabbed a glass of wine for Grace. "Take a sip, it will boost your confidence and help you get a little funkier on the dance floor," he said and handed her the glass.

Grace gulped down her drink. In a very short time, she found herself more talkative and more self-confident. She removed her shoes and let her hair down. Grace took a risk and struck a pose. Everyone laughed, jumped up and down on the dance floor and punched the air singing out loud.

It was almost midnight when Daisy and Lucas arrived home. They were so tired they instantly fell asleep.

***

Lucas woke up before sunrise with a migraine headache. He rolled to face Daisy and placed his arm on her side of the bed. Feeling the empty space, he quickly got out of the bed. He walked into the kitchen and saw her sitting at the table, staring at her laptop screen. Her fingers were flying across the keyboard. Lucas poured himself a glass of water. Daisy was too busy to notice him. He grabbed the old shoebox filled with medicine from the kitchen cupboard. Taking out a blister pack, he removed the pill and swallowed it with some water. Then he sat down next to her. "Good morning, my love. How are you?" He asked.

Her tiny fingers paused over the keyboard. She smiled up at him. "Something inside me is begging me to finish my book. I just can't stop writing, Lucas."

"I'm so happy to hear that. Deep down I knew you would continue your writing. I will support you all the way," replied Lucas. He realised that he didn't feel like a clamp squeezing his skull anymore. Pressure around his forehead and temples was almost gone.

"Thank you, Lucas for being so generous, so kind and so patient. I appreciate your help so much."

"Please let me know if you need anything."

She nodded and continued writing. Lucas made ham sandwiches for himself and Daisy and poured two cups of coffee. "Have a little break, dear. Eat your breakfast to boost your creative energy," he ran his fingers through her hair.

Daisy smiled and gave him a cheek to cheek hug. Lucas ate his sandwich in two bites and finished off his coffee. Throwing his leather jacket over his shirt, he blew an air kiss at her just before he walked out the door, but Daisy didn't notice a kiss through the air. Her busy mind wasn't in the present. She curled up in a chair and closed her eyes. A bright beam of light struck her like a flash of lightning from the sky and she time travelled with her mind.

Daisy found herself sitting on a rock at the exit of the cracked Afghan river bed. Low flying helicopters were zooming around. She covered her ears to block out the loud noises. She noticed a few soldiers hiding in trenches dug into the surface of the rock. One of the soldiers poked his head out of his trench and the bullets instantly started flying in the air. The soldiers began crawling forward on their bellies. They went into the river in an attempt to get to the other side. There were silenced shots as the Afghan soldiers fired bullets into the water.

Daisy had a stabbing sensation in her chest when she saw that the river got covered with blood. All of a sudden, she heard two soldiers talking to each other loudly in Australian accent. She turned her head and saw her father, Harry Barton and his fellow comrade, Noah Irving, hiding behind the rock. Noah ran to pick up a weapon of the dead soldier, but his attempt failed as he got severally wounded in the leg. Harry quickly climbed out of his trench. He threw himself in the path of machine gunfire and ran towards Noah, trying to protect him from the attacker.

Daisy was so scared she felt dizzy. Her breath became quick and shallow. Everything felt so real that she couldn't distinguish between imagination and reality. She watched in horror the sniper aiming to shoot her father down. She wished she could save him, but her legs felt like cinder blocks, making it impossible to move. They were practically glued to the ground. In the blink of an eye, Harry was shot in the back. Stumbling forward slightly, he landed face down in mud.

Daisy felt the shock wave after her father had been hit by the bullet. She felt as if the bullet had entered her body and shattered her bones. She had a buzzing feeling for about fifteen seconds and then the sharp pain set in.

Noah crawled towards Harry and rolled him back over. He checked his pulse, but his fellow comrade was already gone. He roared so loudly; Daisy noticed a newly opened wide crack in the ground. Noah found an old photograph of a woman with a crown braid near Harry's dead body. It was drenched in blood. He put the picture back into Harry's chest pocket and gently closed his friend's eyes with his trembling hand.

Daisy cried her heart out as she saw her father die with her own eyes. She couldn't stop shaking and trembling. The sound of the helicopters faded.

Daisy! Daisy!" she heard her name being called from a far, far distance. She opened her eyes and saw Lucas, staring at her, wide-eyed. "What happened? Why are you crying?" He asked.

Daisy was still trembling inside. Luca's eyes drifted to the plate with the untouched ham sandwich on it. Daisy saw that her laptop keyboard was wet with tears. Wiping her eyes hard with both hands, she gave him a little smile. She felt numbness in her feet after sitting in the same position for too long. She rubbed her feet to get rid of pins and needles prickling sensation and stood up from her seat, but she quickly crossed her legs to stop from wetting herself. She thought her bladder would explode. "I can't hold it any longer," she murmured to herself and rushed to the bathroom.

Lucas could hear the splish splash sound of Daisy's urine pouring down against the ceramic bowel. It was the longest pee she had ever done. When she relieved herself, she gave a deep moan of pleasure.

**

Daisy printed out two hundred pages of her manuscript from her printer. She used a heavy-duty stapler to firmly bind papers together. She was relieved that she managed to convey her own feelings and emotions into her novel. For several months she had carried the seed of new life around in her imagination and now she felt as if she had given birth to her first child. To her surprise, she felt quite tearful and tired. For a moment she stood still, she had a feeling she had gone into a prolonged labour and experienced a lot of pain, but the end result was so worth it. She hugged her manuscript close to her chest like a baby.

"Congratulations on completing your first novel. Not many do," said Lucas and gave her a peck on the lips.

"Thank you, Lucas. I feel like huge bricks have been lifted from my back. I'll be forever grateful to you for the motivation you gave me to face the challenges."

"I guess you took a long car ride and finally reached your destination. Let's have a celebratory glass of wine," said Lucas as he grabbed the wine bottle out of the fridge. Pushing the cork in with the handle of a wooden spoon, he opened the bottle of wine. Daisy listened to the gargling sound of wine pouring. She raised the glass to her nose and took a deep sniff. The fruitiness of the wine teased her tongue when she sipped it. Lucas drank his wine slowly, enjoying its taste. "Oh, I almost forgot that I've got a little something for you," he said and pulled a small box wrapped in a glossy paper out of the front pocket of his denim jacket and handed it to her. Daisy quickly tore apart the paper and pulled out the ballpoint pen with her name engraved on it. "Thank you, Lucas. You are so thoughtful," she gave him a long and tight hug. She sank her face into his chest as though asking him to never let her go.

Lucas pulled her closer and placed his arms around her. He could feel blood flowing in her veins. He leaned to whisper in her ear: "I guess we fit together exactly like puzzle pieces. I'm really infatuated with you, Ms. Barton."

"I live for our love, Lucas. My heart beats ten times faster when I see you," replied Daisy. She couldn't stop blushing.

"I can't wait to get a signed copy of your book," he said, smiling.

Daisy smiled back, showing her pearly white teeth. "I need to pop in the office today and give my manuscript to Ms. Brown in person. I would like to hear her opinion. I have been waiting for this day for so long, Lucas," she said in a euphoric voice.

"I'm sure she will immediately fall in love with your story," he tucked her hair behind her ear. "I'll give you a lift to the office, dear."

"If you don't mind, I would like to take a walk to collect my thoughts and rehearse my words."

Lucas chuckled softly. "Just breathe, you will totally nail it."

The fresh air hit Daisy's face as she stepped out of the apartment building. The light wind tossed her spiral curls into her face, pricking her eyes. She brushed her hair out of her face with her fingers and released a soft laugh. She walked fast, swinging her arms up and down energetically. Her footsteps were in sync with her heartbeat. She held a black leather folder so tightly as if she were holding a rare treasure.

An old memory flashed when Daisy entered the office building. She paused with one hand on the stair rail and glanced around the lobby.

She vividly remembered the day she had a job interview. She recalled how nervous and shy she had felt when Ms. Brown looked at her curriculum vitae.

As if hearing her thought, Ms. Brown's secretary shouted out her name loudly. Daisy ran up a set of stairs to greet her. The secretary's face spread in a welcoming smile. "Your eyes are dancing with joy. Did you win a lottery or something?" She asked with a wink.

"It's so much better than winning a lottery. I finished writing a novel I had been dreaming of for so long."

"Congratulations, Daisy!" Exclaimed the secretary. "Come with me, I'll make a cup of coffee for you."

Daisy followed her with quick steps. Approaching the secretary's desk, she noticed that the cactus had grown taller than she had imagined. Out of curiosity, Daisy gently touched it and got poked by a sharp cactus spine. "Oh!" She gasped. I see our little friend isn't so little anymore."

"Are you okay? Asked the secretary. Her voice was laden with concern.

Daisy nodded. From the look on her face, the secretary could tell that she was in pain. "I feel awful that you have been stabbed by the plant I've grown," she sighed. She found a small tweezer in her bag. "I guess it will be perfect for plucking the stubborn glochids," she said to herself as she started removing the clumps of cactus spine out of Daisy's finger.

"Ouch! That hurts! "Daisy exclaimed and swiftly pulled her hand back.

"Sorry, dear. Please, hold still. It will be over soon."

Daisy closed her eyes and inhaled deeply. The secretary removed cactus needles in a single straight motion. "Voila! It's done," she exclaimed in delight.

"Thank you for your help," said Daisy, rubbing her swollen finger.

"I will bring an ice pack for you." Said the secretary.

"Please don't worry about it. I need to see Ms. Brown now. I'd like to give her my finished manuscript."

"Ms. Brown won't be able to come to the office today. You can leave your manuscript with me. I will pass it along to her."

Daisy felt as if she got pricked by a cactus again. "Sure," she said after a moment's hesitation and put the folder on the desk. She stared at it for a moment, wondering whether she made a right decision.

"Your manuscript will be safe with me," said the secretary with an assuring tone.

Daisy thanked her in appreciation and walked down the corridor. Unlocking the door, she entered the room she felt nostalgic for. She expected the same sort of noise that was in the reception area of an office, but it was so quiet one could easily hear a fly buzzing across the room. Daisy saw Mr. Bloom reading a newspaper at his desk.

Clearing her throat, she greeted him. Mr. Bloom pushed his reading glasses which slid down his humped nose. "If you are looking for your friends, they have gone out for lunch already. They always find a reason to get out of the office," he continued reading his newspaper.

Daisy glanced around the room for a moment as if she had lost something.

"Can I help you with anything?" Mr. Bloom asked and looked at her over the rim of his reading glasses.

"I'm good, thanks," she replied and quickly left the room.

Daisy stepped out of the office building at the same moment Lucas stepped in. Seeing him snapped her out of her thoughts and made her heart skip a little. She stopped and grabbed his arm. "What are you doing here?" She asked in a surprised tone.

"How you can already miss someone when you have been parted for just an hour, I really don't know, but believe me I missed you so much that I couldn't stay at home," Lucas gave her a tight hug with a squeeze.

A whimper of pleasure escaped Daisy's lips.

"Hey, let's take a stroll in the park." Suggested Lucas.

Daisy gave him an engaging grin to express her agreement.

Crossing the road, they walked towards the park. The sun was warm, but a gentle breeze was blowing. The tree leaves were rustling to the tunes of a breeze. Listening to the melody of the wind in the trees put

Daisy in a more relaxed mood. "Look, the tree branches are bent down like cylindrical chimes on a Mark tree." Daisy smiled to herself.

Lucas swept his finger through the length of the hanging branch as if he were playing the chimes on a Mark tree. While entertaining his girlfriend, he noticed a man dressed in a multi -coloured clown costume, selling balloons. He quickly ran up to him and bought two balloons.

Daisy glanced at Lucas with amusement. "I have always liked to celebrate things with balloons. As a kid I used to run towards the houses with colourful balloons out front. I knew that something good was going to be inside," she chuckled at the memory of what she said.

"Let's unleash balloons and release our wishes to the sky," said Lucas as he gave her a red balloon.

Daisy closed her eyes. She focused all her energy and attention on her wish for the future. She imagined the desired goal and opened herself up to gratitude. She spent a few moments feeling of what it would be like to have what she asked for. She knew that the universe was responding to her energy, so she sent positive energy to attract good luck into her life. After a moment of silence, she released a balloon in the air and let the universe make progress with its job. Lucas also let go of his blue balloon. The balloons flew into sky until they couldn't see them anymore.

"What did you wish for, Ms. Barton?" Asked Lucas.

"I will tell you about it when my dream becomes reality." She giggled at the thought.

"And I wish your dream to come true," he replied and pressed his warm lips to hers.

A few days later, Daisy received an email. She let her eyes slide casually to the subject line as if she couldn't care less what it might say. Her heart leapt when she read: 'Offer from publisher.' Daisy caught herself holding her breath while reading an email.

"Lucas!" She screamed so loudly that the neighbours could hear it through the walls.

"What happened?" He Asked, looking puzzled.

"My book got picked up by a publisher. And it's not a mistake. They even wrote a paragraph about why they selected my novel. I guess Ms. Brown submitted my manuscript to the publishing house," Daisy burst into noisy tears of joy.

"Congratulations, my love. I'm so proud of you. I always believed in your potential and now it's time you believe in your own capabilities," said Lucas and without warning, he lifted her high in the air. Daisy's head touched the brass chandelier. She squealed and wrapped her legs around his torso as though she were a koala climbing the eucalyptus. He spun her around the room, laughing.

Their hearty laughter and animated chatter got interrupted by an unexpected phone call. Lucas safely put his girlfriend down on the floor. Daisy quickly unzipped her handbag and grabbed her cell phone. The incoming call was from unknown number, but she answered anyway. She instantly recognized Mr. Bloom's voice. His deep voice had a guttural sound and was produced in the back of his throat. He invited her for an interview about her debut book. Daisy was unable to respond for a few seconds. She felt hesitant about being interviewed as she wasn't ready for it, but Mr. Bloom was too insistent. He tried to persuade her to give a short interview for Ms. Brown's sake. He left her no choice other than accepting the interview invitation.

Lucas watched her thinking through her decision. Daisy shook her head. "Do you think I can get over my fear of interviews?" She asked him with a tremor of uncertainty.

"It's pretty normal to have an interview fear. Answering unpredictable questions about yourself can be very stressful. Follow your gut instinct instead of letting your thoughts take over," he took her hand in his to comfort her. "I guess you just need to be real. Lead with your key points and leave the reporter with something to chew on. Trust me, it will be a perfect opportunity for you to share your message with the public."

His encouraging words made her feel calmer and more centred. "What would I do without you, huh?" She gave him a little smile and rested her head on his shoulder.

The next morning Lucas gave Daisy a ride to the office. "Good luck with your first media interview, my love. Remember, you need to talk in the same way just as you would talk to me." He said in an assuring tone.

"What if I don't like an interview question?"

"Keep in mind that you don't have to tell everything. Just use the bridging tactic and move the conversation away from where you don't desire it to be to where you do," he rolled his eyes and winked at her.

She took a deep breath and got out of the car.

Stepping into the lobby, Daisy was greeted by Mr. Bloom. He was dressed in a well-tailored black suit as if he were on the way into an awards ceremony. He guided her upstairs. Daisy quickly climbed up the stairs, but Mr. Bloom had to pause at every second step to take big gulps of air. Daisy felt his heart rate skyrocket as he had shortness of breath. "Are you okay, Mr. Bloom?" She asked and smiled out of politeness.

He nodded his head twice and loosened his collar and tie. When he climbed to the third floor he gasped with relief. He stepped back for her to walk into the room.

Daisy saw Leo sitting on his desk, swinging his legs back and forth. He hopped off and marched towards her with open arms, but failed in his attempt to hug her. Mr. Bloom swiftly grabbed him by his arm, pulling him in another direction. "I'm sorry, mate, but you have to leave and give us some privacy for like twenty minutes."

Leo glanced at him with a worried frown on his face. "But Ms. Brown won't like me roaming the corridor aimlessly during working hours."

"There is no need to be worried. I will take responsibility for it," said Mr. Bloom firmly. He led Leo out and closed the door.

Daisy sat down in the chair and crossed her arms. She tried to relieve herself from her insecurity by a self-hug. She realised that there was no going back. Mr. Bloom opened his leather briefcase and took out a little black Dictaphone. "Are you ready?" He asked.

Seeing the Dictaphone in his hand gave her an adrenaline rush. Her heart rate started jumping up and down and her breathing became shallow. Daisy coughed gently to clear her throat.

"Yes, I'm ready," she replied and clenched her fists as if she were in a boxing ring waiting for the aggressive opponent to attack her. It felt like a combination of fear, anxiety and excitement all at once. Daisy closed her eyes, gaining her strength. Ding! Ding! She had a feeling she heard the boxing ring bell signifying the beginning of the round.

Mr. Bloom placed the Dictaphone on the desk and made himself comfortable in his chair. "So, at what point can you call yourself a writer?" He shot a question at her.

Daisy paused and thought for a moment, her eyes rolling to the ceiling. "Well, I think if you aren't afraid to wrestle with words and face your own fears to craft something beautiful and painful and bring it into the world then you are a writer," she clutched the armrests tightly, waiting for the next question.

"How did you find an inspiration for your book?"

"My father, Harry Barton set an inspirational example to me. He was gifted with the ability to fall in love. He had written splendid poems, expressing his love for my mother. He loved her so much; he took his love to the grave." Daisy sighed, picturing her father's face in her mind. "He was a brave soldier who saved the life of the wounded comrade in the Afghanistan war. His heroic deeds made me feel proud."

"What was the hardest scene to write?"

Daisy closed her eyes tightly as tears formed. "It was very difficult for me to write a sad death scene of my father. In my mind's eye I saw him fall down to the ground after being shot by a sniper. I even heard the sound of his neck breaking as he hit the ground. I wanted to save him, but I was unable to take a step towards him. I had a feeling my legs and arms were paralysed and I lost the ability to move," her voice didn't have its full sound as it got choked with emotion. "I even couldn't wrap my arms around him and say final goodbye to him," Daisy wiped the tears from her eyes, but failed to supress a sob.

Mr. Bloom handed her a glass of water. "Please, drink this down. It will make you feel better."

Daisy guzzled down the whole glass of water at once. "Do you have any more questions for me?" She asked, drying her mouth with the back of her hand.

"Would you mind if I ask you a few questions?"

"Please, go ahead," she said and crossed her arms again.

Mr. Bloom realised that her lips said 'yes,' but her eyes said 'no.'

"I won't keep you here long, I promise," he said and peered into his notebook to search for another question.

"How do you get into the zone of deep concentration from which your inspiration arises?"

"I find very useful to meditate before I start work. It helps the words and creativity flow. I picture the scenes in my mind and get the spontaneous inspiration."

"Is writing energizing or mentally exhausting for you?"

"Writing is extremely energizing and stimulating once I get the train running. It helps me remove the negative energy from my mind and I feel rejuvenated, but sitting at a computer for many hours has one bad side effect," Daisy had a wide smile on her face like a Cheshire cat. "It makes your butt flatter."

Mr. Bloom grinned at her joke. "Have you already decided what to write next?"

Daisy shrugged her shoulders. "I haven't thought about it yet. I never chase ideas, I guess they come naturally to me. Everything I see and touch reminds me of the idea and then it won't leave me alone until it has my full attention. To be honest writing was the only thing that kept me going in my toughest moments."

"What advice do you have for beginner writers?"

"Be patient, it takes a lot of time and self-discipline to develop your craft. Let go of fear of failure and write for yourself. I think personal experience is the best way to start the writing process. Your memories can recall the details that help you to make your writing more specific.

First and most importantly, you need to believe that the story you are creating is really worth time and energy you are investing into it."

"Thank you for the interesting conversation, Daisy," said Mr. Bloom as he closed the notebook.

"I would like to mention one more thing," Daisy leaned forward in her chair. "I truly feel that I should thank the editor- in -chief, Ms. Brown. I couldn't have pulled this off without her help. Ms. Brown suggested me that I could write a novel. I will never forget her kindness. And there is one more person to whom I need to express my gratitude," Daisy's eyes sparkled at the thought. "My boyfriend, Lucas has been the biggest supporter of my writing. He made me believe that a dream is something more than a thought."

Mr. Bloom stood up from his seat with a satisfied look on his face. Daisy heaved a sigh of relief and rose up. Mr. Bloom gave her a firm handshake. "See, my questions weren't as scary as you thought."

"I think talking to a reporter is like dealing with a cop," Daisy said, smiling.

Mr. Bloom threw his head back and let out a giant belly laugh.

***

Daisy woke up long before dawn. She tiptoed out of the room, trying not to wake up her boyfriend. Snuggling down into the rocking chair on the veranda, she covered herself with a blanket. She was very excited and very nervous that finally the book launch day has arrived and she could introduce her debut novel to the public. She was afraid that if she got very thrilled about it, the universe would notice and take her happiness away from her. Daisy looked up at the sky and prayed to God: 'please, grant me success on my book launch day and remove obstacles in my way.' As soon as she finished her prayer, the dawn broke and she saw the first glimpse of sunlight. The gentle sun's rays touched her cheeks like mother's hands. She instantly felt calm as if God listened to her prayer.

The serenity of her mind was disturbed by Lucas. He poked her with a bramble behind her bare neck. Daisy screamed and nearly fell of the chair. Lucas laughed at her reaction.

"Why is scaring people so funny?" She asked as she raised her eyebrows at him.

Lucas threw his arms around her shoulders. "You are so cute, I'm afraid not to eat you alive."

Daisy smiled a tiny bit. Lucas cupped her face very gently in his hands. "You entered a new stage of your writing career, Ms. Barton. From today your book no longer belongs to you. It belongs to the reader."

She lowered her eyes in a shy manner. He gently stroked her silky soft hair and leaned to whisper in her ear. "There is something I need to tell you, but please, promise me that you won't get mad at me," his voice was pleading.

"What happened?" She stared deeply into his eyes.

"I personally invited your mother to the book launch event," he paused, observing her reaction to the news.

Daisy felt a sharp pain under her left rib at the mention of her mother's name. She took a deep breath to relieve a muscle spasm. Lucas stood there, holding his breath. He was dreading her scold that he had gone behind her back and made the decision, but instead of snapping at him, Daisy opened her arms and gave him a big hug. She let him know she loved him without saying a word. They both felt warm and fuzzy inside. She knew that a sincere hug was worth more than words.

At five o'clock sharp, Daisy and Lucas arrived at a bookstore. The long red carpet was laid out for the book launch ceremony. Daisy squeezed her boyfriend's hand tight. "It still feels a little unreal to me." She murmured.

Lucas smiled softly. "It seems like yesterday when I first saw you in your yellow raincoat and rubber boots. You looked like a cute duckling. I saw a dream in your innocent eyes. I'm so happy that you followed that dream and got your heart's desire."

Daisy's cheeks flushed with pleasure. "The moment I laid my eyes on you, love bloomed in my heart like a flower, Lucas."

Her words put a twinkle in his eyes. He tilted his head down to kiss her hand.

They walked along the red-carpet arm in arm. Her pink accordion pleated dress moved beautifully, giving her walk a bit of elegance. When they entered the bookstore, Daisy stopped for a moment as she saw her book poster propped up against the wall showing a soldier staring at a faded picture of his beloved woman. A small sigh of astonishment escaped her lips. She realised that she was happier than she had even been in her life. Momentarily she closed her eyes to savour a special experience.

The loud click sound of the camera shutter came into her ears and distracted her. She opened her eyes and saw Leo, smiling at her. He was holding a camera and lens like a riffle, cupping the lens in his left hand to eliminate camera shake.

"The event can't happen without a good photographer to capture a moment!" He exclaimed.

Daisy smiled broadly as the camera's flash went off. Her eyes shone with inner happiness. Leo tilted the camera at the angle lower than the eye level, trying to capture her positive energy.

"I need to thank you for giving me an opportunity to host your book launch event. Did you know that it was my childhood dream to hold a microphone in my hand and be a master of ceremony?" Leo stared at her goggle-eyed.

Daisy chuckled quietly, shaking her head. "You are the best, Leo. I'm sure the launch party will be going ahead without a hitch."

Leo grinned and winked, giving his seal of approval.

From the corner of her eye, Daisy saw Mr. Irving approaching her in his wheelchair. He was wearing military medals and ribbons on his uniform on the left. Daisy felt shivers of excitement pulsating through her spine. "Your presence gives me strength, Mr. Irving," she said as she kissed him on the cheek. She noticed her book resting on his lap.

"I feel so happy that you managed to do a great job. You brought the history alive. Good going Kiddo!" He exclaimed with tearful eyes. He took off his medal pinned to his uniform and handed it to her. "You are the winner and the winners deserve their rewards."

"I am humbled by your kind words, Mr. Irving. However, I don't feel comfortable accepting such a meaningful gift."

Mr. Irving didn't let her continue talking. He gestured for her to lean towards him. Daisy moved closer and squatted down in front of him. Mr. Irving pinned a medal on her dress and whispered in her ear. "I will give you a new medal when you finish your second book."

She smiled sweetly and kissed the medal expressing her gratitude and respect.

Daisy took a long survey around the hall, narrowing her eyes. Grace was busy with greeting guests and giving away puzzle piece bookmarks and magnets with the image of the book cover for encouraging curiosity. The bookstore was packed with people, but she couldn't find her mother. She gave a sigh of disappointment and sat down in a red velvet chair.

The guests were sipping champagne while reading the introduction of her book. Daisy observed them carefully, analysing their reactions. They were scanning words in a tempo of fixation and saccades. She knew that the book grabbed their attention within the first line. Daisy glanced to the right from which the high heeled shoes sharp click-clack sound had come. When she saw Ms. Brown approaching her, she quickly rose from her chair. Ms. Brown gave her a piercing stare. "Are you ready to talk about your debut book in front of the audience?" She asked.

Daisy gave a resounding yes to her question. Ms. Brown's mouth twisted into a wry smile. "If you were representing a colour, I think you would be the bright red. I see you are not the colour grey anymore," she said, taking a sip of her champagne.

Daisy smiled in response; she was relieved that Ms. Brown thought she became stronger than the obstacles that tried to break her down.

A few minutes later, Leo came up to her. "Now the guests are expecting to hear from you. You don't have to give a long speech, just keep it light and make it significant."

Daisy nodded her head slowly, her gaze strolled over his face absently. Leo led her towards the stage. He tapped the microphone to check the sound. Hearing nothing, he frowned and spoke into it: 'one, two, three, testing.' Once he adjusted the microphone volume, he began his speech with a melodious sound.

"What a beautiful day it is. I want to thank each and every one of you for being here with us to celebrate the glamorous occasion. After countless hours behind a computer screen, my best friend, Daisy Barton has completed her debut novel. She faced many challenges in the writing process and finally conquered all the obstacles with her determination and patience. Now she is ready to share her story with you. I kindly ask you to give your full attention to her. Please, put your hands together for Daisy," he handed her the microphone and whispered in her ear. "Enjoy yourself and please be careful not to trip on the wires," he took a step back as it was her turn to speak.

The audience clapped and cheered loudly. To her great surprise, Daisy felt calm and relaxed rather than fearful. She gave a large toothy grin. "I'm thrilled to have so many people here with me tonight to celebrate the official release of my debut book. Writing has always been a passion for me. I just feel very fortunate and blessed to have been able to make my childhood dream a reality," she said, holding the copy of her book above her head.

Lucas let out a whoop of joy. He cheered, whistled and clapped, encouraging his girlfriend. It filled her with warmth and energy.

"It wasn't easy writing emotional scenes," Daisy raised her voice, so that everyone could hear her. "When I started the research process for my book, I discovered my family secret and felt emotional scars within me," she gasped. Her mouth went dry. She realised she didn't have spit. She felt like driving a car without any motor oil. "It took me quite a while to get over the pain and feel safe.

My boyfriend, Lucas encouraged me to keep writing and not to give up on my dream. What I'm trying to say is that no matter how bad things get, we should never let fear kill our dreams."

Everyone in the room started clapping rapidly to express their delight. Daisy looked around searchingly until her gaze settled on her mother. She was wearing a sky-blue headscarf pulled tight beneath her chin. It perfectly matched her white trench coat. She looked so elegant and graceful; Daisy couldn't take her eyes off her. She gazed at her admiringly as if she were in a museum calmly beholding beauty. Her mother tilted her head slightly to the side and smiled at her. Daisy smiled back. She opened her book at page fifty -five and started reading an emotionally engaging piece. She offered a detailed description of her mother's reaction when she first saw Harry Barton on the dance floor.

Daisy caught her mother taking a step towards her out of the corner of her eye. She paused in mid-sentence, staring at her. Her mother looked at her with warmth in her eyes. Daisy felt as if she were an infant, studying her mother's face. Her comfort with her grew. She had a feeling she knew the sound of her mother's voice which she had heard in her womb, the taste of her mother's salt and blood, the smell of her skin. She realised that she had a strong craving to be held in her mother's arms. She needed soothing contact of her body. Her mother gazed deeply into her eyes, sending the energy of love. The mother-daughter connection was so powerful they broke down in tears.

Leo immediately grabbed the microphone from Daisy's hand to get past an awkward moment. "Let me once again thank the author for the emotional authenticity," he said as he bowed his head slightly. "Finally, the most anticipating moment has arrived! Now the guests can queue up with their purchased copies of the book to be signed," he exclaimed proudly.

Daisy sipped a glass of water and looked out at the audience, smiling softly. A very long queue built up ahead of the book signing. Daisy got the chance to interact with her fans. When she saw her mother standing in the line, her hands started shaking. She opened the book to the title page and wrote: 'To my mother. I hope you enjoy my debut book!'

Daisy's mother hugged the book tightly close to her chest and disappeared in the crowd. Daisy rose up from her seat, her eyes searching for her mother. In her haste, her feet got caught in the plush carpet, she stumbled back and sank into the chair. She felt dizzy and nauseous as if she were hanging upside down for too long. She heard distant air rushing in her ears. She had a feeling she was holding a seashell up to her ear, listening to the echo of the noise in the air. Daisy gasped, she had trouble keeping her balance. The room was spinning around her.

Grace quickly approached her. "Sweetie, you look so pale. Let me help you freshen up," she gently grabbed her by the arm and led her to the restroom. Grace splashed the cold water on Daisy's face. "Sweetie, are you feeling better?" She asked.

"I still feel dizzy and a bit nauseous," replied Daisy as she scrunched up her face.

"Wait a minute, are you sure you aren't pregnant?"

Daisy paused and thought for a moment. "It is quite possible that I'm pregnant," her cheeks instantly got rosy.

Grace gave a chuckle in response. "I will get a home pregnancy test kit at the pharmacy. Please wait for me here, I'll be right back," she rushed out of the restroom.

The thought of becoming a mother gave Daisy emotional chills. She closed her eyes to reconnect with herself. Her heart rate immediately lowered as she got relaxed. Her inner voice acted like a GPS to guide her and assured her that the positive changes were just around the corner. The internal monologue helped her organize her thoughts that she couldn't speak out loud.

A few minutes later, Grace returned back. Daisy took a deep breath and grabbed the pregnancy test kit. She had a sinking sensation in the pit of her stomach. She sat down on the toilet seat, calculating when was her last period. Her heart leapt when she glanced down at the pregnancy test.

"I'm pregnant, I'm really pregnant! She exclaimed at the top of her lungs. "There is a tiny human being with a beating heart growing in my body who is going to call me mom."

Grace laughed with joy. She was so happy to hear the news. "Congratulations! May God bless you and your little one with good health and happiness."

Daisy rubbed her belly gently. "I figured out what my second book should be about."

Grace grinned from ear to ear and exclaimed: "Motherhood!"

The End